NOTHING TO THE WEDDING

SCARLETT FINN

Also by Scarlett Finn

GO NOVELS
GO WITH IT
GO IT ALONE
GO ALL OUT
GO ALL IN
GO FULL CIRCLE

EXILE
HIDE & SEEK
KISS CHASE

WRECK & RUIN
RUIN ME
RUIN HIM

**THE BRANDED
SERIES**
BRANDED
SCARRED
MARKED

THE FORBIDDEN NOVELS
FORBIDDEN DESIRE
FORBIDDEN WANT
FORBIDDEN WISH
FORBIDDEN NEED
FORBIDDEN BOND

NOTHING TO...
NOTHING TO HIDE
NOTHING TO LOSE
NOTHING IN BETWEEN: ONE
NOTHING TO DECLARE
NOTHING TO US
NOTHING IN BETWEEN: TWO
NOTHING TO SAY
NOTHING TO GAIN
NOTHING IN BETWEEN: THREE
NOTHING TO YOU
NOTHING TO THIS PREQUEL: ONE WILD NIGHT
NOTHING TO THIS
NOTHING IN BETWEEN: FOUR
NOTHING TO DO
NOTHING TO NO ONE
NOTHING TO FEAR
NOTHING TO DENY
NOTHING TO BEAT
NOTHING TO TELL
NOTHING TO IT

**FORBIDDEN
PREQUEL DUET**
ALL. ONLY.
ONLY YOURS

**LOVE AGAINST THE ODDS
STANDALONE COLLECTION**
SWEET SEAS
HEIR'S AFFAIR
RESCUED
MAESTRO'S MUSE
GETTING TRICKY
THIRTEEN
REMEMBER WHEN...
RELUCTANT SUSPICION
XY FACTOR

KINDRED SERIES
RAVEN
SWALLOW
CUCKOO
SWIFT
FALCON
FINCH

MISTAKE DUET
MISTAKE ME NOT
SLEIGHT MISTAKE

LOST & FOUND
LOST
FOUND

**THE EXPLICIT
SERIES**
EXPLICIT INSTRUCTION
EXPLICIT DETAIL
EXPLICIT MEMORY

TO DIE FOR...
TO DIE FOR TRUTH
TO DIE FOR HONOR
TO DIE FOR VIRTUE
TO DIE FOR DUTY
TO DIE FOR LOVE

ONE

HERE'S THE THING about weddings. Not getting married, the wedding part. It's never as straightforward as it should be. Getting married could be straightforward, she knew that from experience. Show up. Say your lines. Cake. As in a piece of cake, simple, not an actual cake.

Okay, so she'd admit her experience was limited. Hers was the only wedding she'd been involved with. Believe it or not, despite it being hers, she'd made very few choices. None, really.

Until now.

Her biggest responsibility?

Spoiler alert: swooping onto the stage to enact a last-minute twist.

Wait for it. The time would come.

The LA Grand Hotel's Platinum Suite was no novelty. How many things had happened to them in that hotel? To her. To her friends. To her lover. Could he still be called that after marriage? Hmm. Hope so.

Going into her bathroom—not the master—she slid back the shower screen and turned on the water while waiting for Casanova to pick up the phone.

Ring. Ring. Ring… Zairn or Tibbs? Place your bets for—

"What did you do?"

Ah, said lover. Good.

"My ex-boyfriend just showed up," Roxie said, her fingers retreating from the shower spray. "In LA. In my Platinum Suite. He was in my bedroom too."

"It's Valentine's Day."

Hmm, her guy was completely indifferent to Porter arriving in LA without notice. Sexy as hell. So secure, so confident in them. Was it weird that their relationship still aroused her? Beyond a level that could be classed as normal? He'd told her numerous times it would always be this way. Damn, she hoped that was true.

"I used to sleep with him, you know? Sex. Someone reminded me today that Porter and I used to do that. Him, actually, he reminded me."

"It's Valentine's Day."

"You don't want to ask how he reminded me?"

"It's Valentine's Day."

Nothing. Not a twitch. Damn, she loved this man.

"Again." A smile slunk to her lips. "Comes around every year. Round and round again, my love."

"You spent it with another man last year."

Greg Hatfield, well remembered.

"And I'll spend it with another man this year too. Tripp's promised to dance with me all night. My ass won't hit the couch, so he says. A promise is a promise. I'll hold him to it. I mean, he'll let other men hit on me, of course, your little protégé is a loyal servant."

Again, he stayed on track. "Tell me to get my ass to your door."

Bounced right off.

"No," she said, boosting herself up to sit on the vanity. "We don't need bullshit, exploitative, capitalist carnivals to celebrate our love. I celebrate it every day." Nice, that was nice, even if she thought so herself. "That's why I send you naked pics every day, baby. Proof of love in full living color."

"Almost every Rouge venue holds Valentine's events."

"And we make a mint. Capitalism rocks. We can exploit other people, just shouldn't let ourselves be exploited."

"We shouldn't? We can afford to be exploited."

"You can't leave New York anyway because you have your legacy board to corral."

"It's not my legacy board; we don't own Gramercy." Yep, she was aware. "Reid and Kintyre bought Kinloch out. I'm surplus to requirements."

And if that were true, he wouldn't be so caught up in it all. "You are not. Kintyre's wife just birthed a tiny human. You've met him, the squishy little wriggly thing people keep putting in your arms, remember? He's named after you."

"Oh, right, the baby! I forgot, that's why I'm here."

Talk about exploitation, that sarcasm was ripe for the picking… Resist. Resist. Should be points for staying schtoom.

"Kintyre's priorities are elsewhere." As they should be. "It's sexy when you fight for your friends. Do a good job, might get you laid."

"Reid's got this. If need be, he can call Gauge. This is the kind of shit Gauge does in his sleep."

"And we all know what you do in your sleep," she teased.

"You."

However that worked.

"He's looking good, by the way, Gauge, Rainie's good for him." Leaning back against the mirror, she tucked her feet up on the marble edge beneath her. "I love seeing my girls tame your guys. And he gets jealous too. Gauge needs to spend more time with Tripp, Original Junior isn't a threat to any relationship. You ever heard of him poaching another man's girl?"

With Tripp's revolving door of women, they often referred to him as Junior, to Zairn's senior. Problem was, now they did have a little Zairn Junior in the family. Zay-Jay—as he'd come to be called colloquially—may only be two weeks old, but he was already a priority in so many lives.

"Trouble is, Lo, when a guy poaches, they're often expected to stick with the girl."

And Tripp was definitely a Teflon kind of guy.

She exhaled. "If only he'd get over himself."

"Tripp?"

"Yes, Tripp. He'd be good at sticking if he just got out his own way. Why won't he stick?"

"No idea, Lo. He's a mystery."

No, he wasn't. Frustration fueled the question, it was supposed to be rhetorical. "You don't…?" She frowned. "You know why Tripp is like he is, right?"

"Because variety is the spice of life?"

On a tsk, she shook her head. "Men! How do you miss the glaringly obvious? It's a useless skill, yet you're all experts."

"Tell me."

"No," she said, folding her arm between her legs and body. "I won't do your homework for you. Try studying instead of staring down my dress every chance you get, jock."

"Can't resist my Lola Bunny."

One of his best qualities.

"Tripp will get there," she said. "In his own

time."

"Happens to the best of us."

"Don't you think it's funny when men react to Tripp like he's a threat? Says more about them than it does about him. Says more about their relationships too."

Being the guy typically making other men jealous with his presence, it probably wasn't so funny to Zairn. In fairness, her Casanova could be a threat to others' relationships if he wanted to be. Except with her, and their wedding, in his life his motivation on that score was lackluster to say the least.

"Want me to react to him spending Valentine's with my girl?"

"How about this…" she said, curving her free hand around her bent knee. "I'll spend tonight dancing with Tripp…"

"Yeah?"

"And in less than two weeks, I'll marry you."

"Slight flaw in that statement, Lo."

With a roll of her eyes, her head bumped back on the mirror. "Well, yeah, but go with it, Skippy. How about in less than two weeks, I'll walk down the aisle to you. Is that better? I'll wear a floofy dress and get my hair done, may even shave my legs—I haven't decided."

"Nervous yet?"

She almost laughed. "It's weird, isn't it? People ask that all the time. I get it from my Delights, the Crimsettes, not just fans and strangers, I get it from people we know too. Real life people. Why do they ask that?"

"I don't know. For something to say? Maybe it's normal for other people."

"To be nervous? Why would anyone marry someone they didn't love and trust completely?"

"Because not all people are lucky enough to have

the perfect partner."

This time, her smile liberated the laugh. "Tripp told you about that, huh? Tattletale. He's supposed to have a woman's back. You really shouldn't talk too much to my friends."

"*Your* friends? I've known that kid since he was a pimple-faced brat who couldn't string two words together in front of a woman. Who do you think taught him the secrets?"

"So his perfection is Zairn-induced?"

"I was a different man before you, you know that?"

Though she sometimes played up the contradiction, she loved how her guy was always half a step away from sappy.

"Are you getting romantic on me?"

"Blame it on the alcohol."

Yeah, 'cause it was likely he'd hit the bottle at that time of the morning during back-to-back meetings. Regardless of the latter, if she asked him to get on a plane, he wouldn't hesitate for a second.

"Our wedding is in twelve days."

"Yes, it is."

"Jane's having kittens."

"Yes, she is."

"Baby on one coast, wedding on the other. It's an embarrassment of riches," she said. "The house isn't ready yet."

"I heard."

"Turns out sometimes you can't just throw money at a problem."

"It will all work out."

Some might think it was a wonder they could be calm with so many things in limbo. Yeah, okay, they didn't have to chase the details of their wedding day because Jane, her BFF, was doing that for her. That didn't leave them off the hook completely.

Remember the twist? It required preparation and deception, at least for now.

"We have to keep her busy," she said. "It's not cruel."

"No."

"Talk to Knox?"

"Most every day."

"Is he nervous?"

Zairn laughed. "He's a Collier, babe. There's no such thing as a nervous Collier."

"Cam's in town."

"He come to the club last night?"

"More to see Tripp than me."

"Disappointed?"

"I hid it well," she said. "I have errands today."

"You told me."

"Errands feel… beyond me."

"Nothing is beyond you, Roxanna."

"This kind of thing. Wedding errands."

"Jane's made all the big decisions," he said, "just make the necessary tweaks. You're doing it *for* her."

"Ranks are still closed, right?"

"You, me, Knox, Ballard."

"And Toria."

"And Toria."

"Told Tripp yet?"

"Do you know how hard it is to keep a secret from that guy?"

"Especially when you're drinking with him every night. You're strong, Lola. His usual tactics don't work with you."

"You hope they don't work," she teased with no sincerity. "This is the right thing. We're doing the right thing."

"Hey, the rest of us are too busy being astounded

you and Knox agree on something."

"We agree that Beautiful Jane gets whatever she wants." Arching her back, her feet slipped from the vanity. "This means the world to her. It's exciting, I can't wait to see her face. She may just pass straight out, maybe we should push the guests' arrival an hour. Give her time to rebound."

"You and Knox have this. I have complete faith in both of you."

"Says the guy who only has to show up. If you want to that is. Amount of money this thing cost, it's happening no matter what, just so you know. If you change your mind, don't cancel, jilting me at the altar is completely fine. I told Bastian we'd put names in a hat and pick some guy at random to take your spot if you don't show up."

"Could land on Blayne."

She shivered. "Don't even joke about that. And now you know why Roman didn't get an invite. One way or another, I'll be getting married that day."

"Why'd you think we settled on LA, Lo? You love getting arrested over there."

"Least this time it wouldn't be on you to bail me out."

"You didn't consider that one of the people responsible for getting me there is Ballard?"

"Ballard loves me. He has to, he's no fool, I know where the bodies are buried. Jilt me and I'll put everything on blast."

"Guess I have to show up then."

"Guess you do."

The door opened enough to let Tripp poke his head in. "Need my phone."

"Uh, I'm naked in here."

She wasn't but could be, he didn't know.

"Uh huh," he said without reacting. "That your

guy? Tell him to buy you a damn cellphone."

"I'm sending Astrid," Zairn said in her ear.

"No, I don't need Astrid, I…" Hmm, wedding errands. "Yes, send Astrid."

"Finally you learn to follow orders," Zairn declared. "I put her on a plane two hours ago."

"You put her on a plane?"

"Me, Tibbs, it's details, babe. I love how you're falling in line. Marriage is good for us."

She scowled at no one. "This is not compliance, it's kindness. Astrid prefers being with me than she does you. With you oozing that charisma all over the place and looking the way you do—which is kind of rude, by the way, around such a young, impressionable woman. You should really stop that."

"I'll look into it. In the meantime, remember it's her cousin's primary mission to ensure my safety. Not likely I'll start screwing around in the family."

"It is not," she said, waving Tripp away when he came in, hand outstretched. "Ballard's primary mission is to keep me safe." She grinned. "Tripp's growling. I'll call when he's done being impolite."

"Love you, Lo."

"I love you too, Casanova." Though she stretched out every word in the sentence, Tripp did let her get it out before snatching the phone. "You're rude."

"Says the woman who creeps into my room at night to steal my phone."

"No one important called. You're not as popular as you think. Though one woman did cry when I said I was your wife."

"Could've been my mother."

She shrugged. "Could have been."

Unlikely because his mother was sitting in their suite's living room with her best friend, but Alice Breckenridge certainly would bawl, happy tears, if her fun-loving son settled down.

He started to turn away, already typing into the phone.

"No. No. No," Roxie said. "Stay there, I need the phone back, I have to talk to Z about Porter and Crosby."

A subject her lover managed to erase from her mind. That was the problem with their conversations, often they went off on their own tangents. Maybe that was why they ended up talking fifty times in a day.

Still typing, Tripp gestured slightly toward the running shower. "If you're getting in there, I'm leaving the room."

Good point. She wouldn't shower with her brother in the room either.

"Okay, but don't go too far. We have wedding errands today."

That brought his slow blink up from the phone. "Wedding errands? Yeah, that doesn't sound like my thing. My mom is here. It's her thing. Carolyn's too."

Carolyn Hunt was Alice Breckenridge's lifelong BFF. She liked people with BFFs. Was instantly something they had in common.

"Okay, fine," she stated, "but when it comes around to secret telling time, I'll know who to leave out the loop."

"Secret telling? Which secret? Secrets like that you and Z got married last summer? Or that the next wedding's actually a twofer. Jane doesn't know that your wedding day is her wedding day too. She'll be up at that altar with Knox saying her vows right alongside you and Zairn."

Uh, spoiler alert!

With a wink and a flat smile, he turned and marched on out, typing again.

"We won't name our kids after you!" she called

out. Shock became a sigh. "You know, I'm not surprised. Our Pretty, Little Priest has his ways. Hmmm…" Her eyes narrowed. "How does he do that?"

TWO

"THE WHOLE THING shouldn't take too long," Roxie said, Alice and Carolyn at her flanks.

Tripp stayed in the suite. Of course. Even his mother didn't try to persuade him to come along. He'd only end up flummoxing the coordinator anyway.

Up ahead, two security guys blocked the ballroom's doorway until their trio was within a few feet. Only then did they step aside to open the doors. Inside, a flurry of people dashed this way and that, around various pieces of furniture and tables loaded with wedding accoutrements.

"Ms. Kyst…" From the center of the room, a woman with an earpiece and a tablet came rushing over. As the identity of Roxie's cohorts registered, said woman's expression became something more… insecure. "Mrs. Hunt. I… I didn't realize you'd be joining us today."

"Hmm, I probably should've thought twice about bringing the owner's mother with me," Roxie said. "She's not the only one with power, I could get you fired too, you know."

"Oh, Roxie," Alice said, smiling at the coordinator. "Please, ignore Carolyn and I, this is Roxie's day." Sort of. "What's your name?"

"Kym. Everything is under control."

"There's a lot going on," Roxie said, scanning the workers. "Is there another wedding this week?"

"Oh, no, this is all for you and Mr. Lomond," Kym said. "Will he… join us?"

"Unlikely 'cause, last I heard, he's in New York." Adjusting her focus, Roxie waved the question away. "He doesn't care about this stuff. If he was here, he'd be too busy hitting on you to pay attention. You've seen the news, right?"

Of his affair. With a woman he'd never met, by the way. An inconvenient truth the media didn't care about. Talk about irrelevant details being sacrificed to sensationalism.

"Roxie," Alice chastised, still wearing that smile. "She's joking. None of the rumors are true."

Though she may not reveal that to Reeve Crosby later when giving him a quote. Something she was still cooking up. Shame her and Casanova hadn't talked again. Good thing he was used to her surprises.

"Well, uh, I can say everything is under control here," Kym said, backing away a few steps to gesture to the end of the room. "On the day, we'll have all the pocket doors open to the back courtyard, where the ceremony itself will take place. Seating will be in here, and we'll open the two quadrants beyond to accommodate your numbers."

"Where did those land in the end?"

"Immediate family and friends only. Final RSVPs take us to one thousand three hundred and seventy-three."

Whoa, hey, back it up, what now?

Her mouth opened and activity around them ceased, it was possible she'd cursed rather loud. With her ears ringing, it wasn't totally clear.

"A thousand and—I had like seven people on my list! And Blayne was more of a maybe."

This was what she got for not paying closer attention. Intimate. That's what she'd said to Zairn when they first talked about it. More than a thousand bodies didn't sound intimate… Could be a lot of fun though. Would be interesting either way.

"We do expect there will be a few additional guests on the day."

"And some no-shows?"

That had to be obvious.

She could find a way to divert people at the airport… that would require a cunning plan. Send them to a dummy wedding, maybe? Capers were so much more fun with like-minded allies. Why wasn't Toria in LA with her? Oh, yeah, because her friend was in the trenches in New York, keeping Jane occupied and rerouted, if necessary.

"Unlikely," Carolyn said, passing them to check something out in more detail. "It's a popular event. If people have RSVP'd, they're coming."

Yeah, billionaires were like that. If they didn't want to be somewhere, they weren't there, and didn't shy from saying it. Polite wasn't high on the list of considerations.

Thank God this was Jane's wedding too. She'd be happy to address the crowd and do the public speaking thing, but if the masses wanted a gooey bride, Jane would fill that quota.

"Numbers will at least double for the late après reception off-site. Mr. Ballard assures us security will be tightly controlled."

"It's just Ballard," she said. "You don't need the

mister. And security is all him. He's got that."

Especially knowing he'd brought in Ryder Stone's firm along with the Breckenridge brothers security specialists.

"What are you worried about?" Kym asked. "Perhaps I can alleviate your concerns."

"I'm not worried about anything." With Jane at the helm, worry was completely unnecessary. "Just figured I should show my face and—one thousand people in the same room?"

You know what it was? Knox. It was him. The middle Collier brother getting married would be a sight to see. Though, huh, people would say the same thing about Zairn. And her, though her pool was smaller. Way, way smaller.

Only problem with that argument was Jane didn't know the guests were for her wedding too. Knox must've nudged her into inviting people he'd want there, right? Helped that he and Zairn had known each other forever. The Collier clan were Zairn's clan too. And, on top of that, Jane's people were her people, so they'd all be invited either way. No one would be left out.

Man, they were smart. Sneaky? Yes. But, God, it was going to be fun. Drama at the wedding of the century, people would expect nothing less. It was her job to satisfy those appetites.

"Does everyone just sit where they want?" she asked.

"Oh, no, there's a strict seating plan, Ms. Kyst. For here and the meal."

"We're feeding a thousand people too?"

"Miss Simmonds has taken care of the food arrangements for the reception. After the ceremony, there will be a second drinks reception before the formal meal here. Transport has been laid on to move people from here to the club after hours. Logistics are meticulous. Every eventuality has been accounted for."

Inspecting the space, she couldn't see it. "How do you feed a thousand people in here?"

"The other quadrants are other ballrooms, the whole thing can be opened up into one large room. And we have a second tier…"

That took her attention upward.

"Are we opening the mezzanine?" Carolyn asked.

"For the drinks receptions, yes. Not for the ceremony. Only security will be allowed upstairs during that."

"We also have an overspill space beyond the courtyard, if needed…" Carolyn said. "Pictures?"

"In the courtyard and on the bluff." Oh, there would be pictures too. "We have taken precautions against unsanctioned access. There will be drones and people on the roof."

"On the roof like…?" Oh! Exciting! "Am I finally getting my sniper?"

Alice laughed, Carolyn was just as amused, Kym didn't seem sure how to take the question.

"We set up broad reflectors and prohibit anyone from flying overhead to access the courtyard. And we have canopies that will be erected before the helicopters move the wedding party from here to the après reception."

Helicopters. Huh. "Jane doesn't like helicopters." Meaning she may try to avoid that mode of transport. She'd have to talk to Knox. "I need to see the seating plan and transport schedule."

"Okay," Kym said. "Miss Simmonds has—"

"Yeah, I'm the bride, I get to override her decisions. I also get to tell you not to tell Miss Simmonds or we'll take our business elsewhere."

People didn't often expect her to crack out no-

nonsense-Roxie, but this was maybe the most important thing she'd done in her life so far. Jane had done so much work putting all of this together, far more than she'd realized. Her BFF took her role seriously, and Roxie would too. Jane deserved the world, and it was on her to make damn sure her friend got it.

THREE

ROXIE MADE HER excuses when Alice and Carolyn invited her to join them for shopping and lunch. She couldn't accept their promise to make a day of it because she had a prior engagement.

The Platinum Suite's butler—who they wouldn't normally have around when Zairn was in charge—brought her guest inside.

"Ms. Kyst," the butler said, stepping aside to gesture at the other man. "Reeve Crosby."

Pasting on a smile, she opened her arms. "We don't need to be introduced." The butler was already departing. "We're old friends, Reeve, right?"

"Always happy to get your call, Roxie."

Funny, given it had only happened once.

"Shame I can't say the same." Her smile stayed in place and her tone amicable. She didn't give his twitch of confusion time to fully manifest and just sailed on. "Please come sit down."

This was nice. Polite. Friendly. She could be personable when required. The press didn't always get that side of her. She wasn't openly hostile… often. Zairn called it a "symbiotic relationship." Yeah, the media had done them favors, and it was easier now she had a hold of steering. Being a passenger was much less fun. Her guy wasn't wrong though. She should listen to him more often. What was she thinking? There was no one she trusted more. But that ego of his had to be kept in check, couldn't let him get any big ideas…

She and Reeve sat at opposite ends of the same couch, and she poured coffee from the pot on the table. Gracious. Placid. Completely non-threatening. No claws needed. Not yet anyway.

"Heard Zachary Kintyre had his kid," Reeve said. "Got any pictures?"

"Oh, yeah, hang on while I send you a dozen."

She paused and tipped her chin his way, showing a smile that countered his. They both knew there were pictures, and they both knew she wouldn't share them.

"Can't blame a guy for trying."

Couldn't she? She finished pouring and handed him a cup.

"His wife had more to do with producing the kid than he did."

"She's great. Lilya's great."

"Yes, she is." She settled back. Enough small talk, this was no dilettante's luncheon. "We have business."

"Yes, we do." He produced a tablet from his messenger bag. "I haven't had a lot of time with this. I didn't know you were going to call—though I love that you did. You can. Any time. I almost brought Beverley with me but—"

"Beverley Woo?"

The producer. Interesting.

"She's the best way to get to Karryn Keller." Super famous top-tier TV interviewer. "You want the best. You deserve the best."

Oh, did she? Nice of him to notice. Though the opinion may change when he wasn't buttering her up.

"I think there's been a misinterpretation."

"What do you mean?" he asked, unlocking his tablet.

Before he could get as far as opening any app, she slid closer to push the device down. "I didn't invite you here to ask questions, I invited you here to answer them."

And his brow lowered. "Answer them?"

"Anjelica."

"I don't know her." He was quick to shake his head though had an air of reveling in the reversal of roles. Her Casanova wasn't the only one with an ego. "I could try to…"

"I'm not interested in you trying anything."

"I'm surprised Zairn's still in New York. Thought he'd get here as fast as he could after the story broke."

She sipped her coffee. "Why would he do that?"

"Haven't heard anything about the wedding being canceled."

"Ah, is that why you rushed over here? You want the scoop? Is this where I confess all?"

"You must've thought about calling the wedding off."

Must've? No. In private, months ago, she and Zairn discussed stepping aside for Jane's special day, giving all the focus to her friend. If their wedding, hers and Zairn's, was ever to be called off, or they decided not to go ahead with it, that would be a decision made together. Never apart.

Helped that they were already married.

That might be a closely held secret, meaning it wasn't often addressed, but she couldn't imagine not having that security cradling her through life. Now it was there, she wouldn't be able to live without it.

Maintaining her confidence, she faux sighed. "Oh, Mr. Crosby, you should do better research. Didn't you see my stream last night?"

"From the club?" He put the tablet on the table and settled back. "Looked like you were having a good time."

"I was." She set the cup on the table. "I always have a good time in Crimson."

"With a Breckenridge."

Reporters wanted information, that was their stock and trade, she got it. They weren't used to being the providers of information, which may be why he didn't realize this was going exactly the way she assumed it would. There was no trust, only mutual satisfaction… or dissatisfaction.

"Yes," she agreed, "a Breckenridge. A whole one all to myself. Greedy? There's enough to go around."

"Tripp Breckenridge has a reputation."

"So I've heard."

"You spend a lot of time with him."

"And you think maybe Zairn is jealous or wants rid of the young scallywag?"

"He's a man used to attention. You and Breckenridge are closer in age, kindred spirits. Zairn's ready to settle down."

"Tell you that himself, did he?" Tossing her hair, she turned more toward him. "Zairn knows what he wants."

"What is that?"

Her smile was unashamed. "Me."

"Thinks he can have you and his sidepiece too?"

"We're talking about Zairn Lomond here."

Interest raised his chin. "Meaning?"

"You know what I mean."

Generalities were okay. And he could make his assumptions and reach his own conclusions.

"That you accept it? Him and other women? That he can handle two of you. More than two? What do you get out of the deal if he keeps on with the lifestyle? Suiting himself?"

The cretin was almost salivating. A private audience. For him, it was probably better than hardcore porn.

"You want me to say words that will justify our lives."

"Is it the money?" he asked. "The exposure? Is the relationship even real?"

"Why would you ask that?"

"You spend a lot of time apart. Now we find out he has this girl on the side—or is he responding to the obviously intimate relationship you have with Tripp Breckenridge?"

"Obviously?"

"You're not alone. He keeps his options open. A lot of women fall for it."

Her half smirk wasn't easy to subdue. "Fall for… Who are we talking about now?"

"Breckenridge."

"Any one in particular?"

"This is your story, Ms. Kyst. You came into Zairn's life… things haven't been the same since then."

She filled her lungs. "The same for who?"

"Zairn. His life. The people in it. Public perception. It's no secret there are those who doubt your sincerity."

"Do you doubt my sincerity?"

"It's not my job to judge."

"You're just the messenger?"

"Tough job, but someone has to do it."

She didn't believe for a second that he was

humble or modest.

"Whatever it is you're trying to say, Reeve, say it."

"I get it. You want the man for the lifestyle and credibility he can give you. In exchange, you improve his image by overtly displaying a relationship. While in the background he…" She could tell he anticipated her filling in the blank. She didn't, just folded her arms. "You know… you're a beard."

"Oh, is that what I am? Didn't your momma teach you it's not nice to call people names?"

"I'm on your side, Roxie. You were plucked out of nowhere. You didn't ask for this. The life you lived before is gone. You can't fade into obscurity now, people are too invested. He has you." Damn right. "Fans, Zairn lovers, even Zairn haters, are intrigued by you. This is where you are, and you have to make the most of it."

"Is that what I'm doing?"

"You tell me," he said. "What's really going on here? Is it really going to happen?"

"The wedding?"

"It's a big commitment if you're not invested."

"What makes you think I'm not?"

"You have pride. This man's making a fool of you. He's having an affair."

"What makes you so sure?"

"I don't have to be sure," he said, almost shrugging her off. "I'm not the one walking down the aisle in eleven days."

"Twelve."

"I've heard he's got a week of bachelor parties lined up in various states."

"Heard from who? Did you get an invite?"

He snickered. "My source is robust."

"That tells me a lot."

"Zairn's had a wild life. I'm surprised Anjelica's

the first woman to sell her story since you got together."

"Yes, that is curious."

Reeve wanted to probe, to ask, to delve deep. As he almost leaned in, she was surprised he didn't need the tablet to hide his arousal.

"Have you heard stories? Had women getting in touch? I could help."

Her head tilted. "Help? How?"

"You want to be sure he's committed. That he won't make a fool of you." Hmm. Okay. Stay quiet because he'll keep going in just a few—"There have to be other women. You've known each other eighteen months now." His smirk was close to ridicule. "Eighteen months! You don't honestly think he's been faithful to you all that time. Zairn Lomond? Monogamous?"

She didn't have to "think" it because she knew it wholly and completely.

"What do you suggest?"

"I'll do some digging. Ask some questions. I can get you answers."

"You can…" She better be selling this. "No, I—"

"I've never done you wrong, Roxie." Hadn't he? "No one has to know, we'll keep it between us."

Pretending to ponder, she rolled her lips between her teeth. "Reeve—"

"I'll get Anjelica. I'll find out what happened, where she came from, who found her…"

"Who found her is something I've wondered myself."

"Do you think she's finished? That she'll disappear now?"

"I don't know, Mr. Crosby. Why don't you tell me?"

"I can find out."

"Who paid her? Who set her up to rear her head

at this opportune moment?"

"I can find out."

"Really," she said, sliding along the couch. "You can find out?"

"Yeah," he strutted. "Maybe it's not about money. If money was it, she'd have contacted Zairn. Told him how much she was being offered…" Blackmail. "And he'd have given her more to keep her quiet." Another frown. "Unless he's playing to it. Could be he's goading you. Showing the world he's got you right where he wants you."

Uh huh. Oh, it wasn't easy to restrain her incredulity. Was he honestly expecting her to buy his innocence and Zairn's guilt? He might think he was getting in, and she'd keep on letting him believe that.

Exuding uncertainty, innocence faded up. She couldn't play it too hard or he'd know she was messing with him.

"I don't know…"

"Don't be naïve," he said, inching nearer.

"Naïve?"

"What's the harm? Think about it. If there's nothing to find, you've got peace of mind."

Raising her thumbnail to her teeth, she worried it just a little. "Hmm, there's just one little problem."

"What's the problem?"

Pushing the tablet along the couch, out of her way, she kept on going until her knee touched his thigh.

"Maybe I'm not so…" Her thumb trailed down her throat, over her breast, descending from her body until her crooked forefinger could touch his leg. "Innocent myself."

The flash of his surprise betrayed him being caught on the spot. "You're saying you…?"

"We've never had a chance to get to know each other, properly, you and me." Her finger slid further across his leg to join the others. "Would you like to get to know me, Mr. Crosby?"

"I… I don't…"

Widening her smile again, she leaned in a little. "If you think for one second I don't know you're behind the Anjelica bullshit, you're sadly mistaken. You stir the pot, Reeve. You stir and stir. Anything for the story. You've sucked that innocent woman into the mud and she won't thank you for it in the end, I guarantee it."

"Roxie, I would never—"

"Print whatever the hell you like, but don't you ever doubt Z to my face again. Don't do it when I'm in the fucking room. I guarantee you'll regret it."

"I—"

Strengthening her legs, she shot to her feet. "Get the hell out of my sight."

Scrambling up, he was quick to turn on his heels and run the hell out of there. As the suite door closed, Tripp appeared from the internal hallway, still mussed from bed but dressed at least.

"Who was that?" he asked.

Obviously he'd heard the door close.

On an exhale, she sat again and swept up her coffee. "No one important."

"Rox Out, what are you doing?"

"Nothing," she said, aware he'd never buy her innocence so ended it with a sly smile. "Just entertaining myself."

He nodded to the seat beside her. "What's that?"

Ah, look at that, Reeve had been so desperate to leave, he'd forgotten his tablet.

She swept it up. "This is Dyce tech."

"And Rourke's Mosaic software."

Oh, he read her mind.

"Think I'll give Roux a call," she said. "Maybe we'll take a trip north."

"They're not back home until tomorrow."

She hadn't even known they were anywhere.

"How do you know that?" she asked.

"Mieux's holding things together up there." He dropped onto the couch beside her, taking the tablet at the same time. "Your friend won't come back for it?"

"He could try, but my guess is we're safe. I don't think he'll be bothering us for a while."

FOUR

ROUX RADLEY-ROURKE was one of her favorite people. Sure, she had a lot of favorite people, but Roux was up there as the queen of badass and sass. Rourke, so-called "man of the house," was the kind of guy who played up to irritating everyone. He didn't shy from antagonizing people, from saying the controversial thing. These days, a lot of that skill was directed at his wife, Roux. For the couple, every word was foreplay in action. Hmm, she could identify with that.

The couple had a custom-built house on a large compound that also contained two businesses and Zane Dyce's house. The place was like a retreat—with every comfort known to man.

"We should probably just give it back," Roxie said, the rogue tablet on the kitchen island next to their bottle of wine. "That would be the polite thing to do."

"Who gives a fuck about polite?" Roux asked.

"I didn't plan to rake through the whole thing. Would like to prove he rounded up this Anjelica woman though. I can't stand the thought of someone exploiting a person like that."

"Reeve Crosby is an asshole. He deserves it. Tripp will drag Hotshot back here and we'll dig in deep. Could be all kinds of embarrassing stuff on there. Wonder if Crosby would like to be the subject of his own news bonanza."

"You think the world would care?"

"As much about his private life as yours? No. They're smarter than that. That doesn't mean putting it out wouldn't be embarrassing." And it does help that we have access to the CollCom microphone." Roux picked up her wine. "Or you do. I promised Knox I'd never call him again unless Rourke was dying."

"If you needed an alibi? Girl, you call me if you need a witness to get on the stand."

"The promise was less about the dead and more about the not calling him."

Roxie raised her wine glass. "Here's to our humiliation eclipsing theirs."

The affinity they'd always share.

"You'd think Knox would be smarter than to fall for that shit."

"Right?" Roxie asked as Roux's glass tinged on hers.

As they drank, their eyes met. Knox Collier was instrumental to both of their relationships being on their current courses. Knox accommodated both of their reunions with the men in their lives, the men they loved. And, thinking about it, he didn't actually get anything in return.

Until now. Satisfaction came with their cunning plan. Yeah, she and Knox drew glares off each other whenever they got the chance, but she loved him, like a brother. They were family.

Giving Jane her special day might be the main objective, but Knox deserved his happily ever after too.

And, damn him, so much of his happiness came from seeing Jane's that Roxie couldn't honestly dislike him. Had she told him that? No. Should she?

"I'm not going to ask if you're nervous about the wedding because I know you better than that," Roux said, topping off their glasses. Finally someone got it. "Doesn't the wedding feel like this big… thing?"

"A spectacle? I'm okay with that. It's Zairn Lomond for crying out loud, I have to break hearts across the world or those hos might think they have a chance with him."

"Who's to say they don't?" Roux asked. "I'd lease Rourke out for the right price."

"You have access to his bank account, you don't need money," Roxie said. "So barter? Or do you mean if he pisses you off too much?"

"He pisses me off every day and I have yet to find any takers. We'll never know."

"You ever sorry you did it the way you did?"

"Getting married? No. Not even a little bit. Shit, Rourke and I are not the 'stand up in front of people' types. We would, it's not like we're short of confidence, but you know how he likes to show off."

"And you like to bait him."

"That too." Roux gestured with her glass. "We'd be up there all day trying to one up each other." Or they'd go at it right there. One would push the other until… "It would be an endurance marathon. We'd have to pay people to show up, provide hydration and power bars. No way am I spending that much of my kids' inheritance."

Of every couple in their group, Roux and Rourke were the only ones to state they didn't want kids. Was that decision permanent? Who knew? Though they did get pretty wrapped up in each other. Could be that the kids would be forgotten in particular moments, the ones that got the couple hot. DCFS tended to look down on neglect in deference to sex, or so she'd assume.

Although… they could pay for a nanny, a squad of them. Pay? Yes. But would it be enough? They'd need a new road straight from their house to court, or a helipad on the roof. With the couple's penchant for exhibitionism, they'd probably end up hopping from one sexual harassment suit to another. Would anyone ever be touched or coerced? No, only husband to wife and vice versa.

The tablet flashed, then the screen went blank. Damnit, had Crosby disabled the thing from afar? If he could do that, what took him so long?

Words leaped to the screen.

HOTSHOT: WHY IS THERE AN UNKNOWN DEVICE TRYING TO CONNECT TO MY NETWORK?

"You, you and your network," Roux barked at the screen. "So frickin' precious."

"Is that…?"

"My beloved? Oh, yeah, guy can't keep his snout out a conversation." Again her ire landed on the tablet. "We can't respond to you, fool, the thing is locked. It's probably poisoned and—"

The screen flickered and there it was, the home screen. Oh, God.

"How did he do that?" she asked. "Is it—"

"Impressed, Kyst-meister?"

Rourke strolled on in, well, more like swaggered. Arrogance wasn't a big enough word, though he always wore enough of a smirk to betray he didn't really take himself that seriously. That was one of the reasons she loved him. Who had time to be offended left and right?

"She's not impressed," Roux said. "Neither of us are impressed, Hotshot."

When Tripp came in not long after, the parade of the cocky and blessed was almost comical.

"How many more of you are there?" she asked. "This wedding's going to be a meat market."

Roux opened her arms when Tripp came over to kiss her, then the two hugged. "You've been hiding."

"Never stay still," Tripp said. "Always got somewhere to be."

"Where do you have to be now?" Roux asked, handing him her wine.

After drinking some, he gave back the glass. "Here. And that's warm."

"I know," Roux said and landed a glare on the man opening the fridge. "Someone filled the shelves with his special, revered beer and I couldn't be bothered going downstairs. Rox and I are troopers. We rally."

And had lived most of their lives in a lower tax bracket… a much lower tax bracket. And in that bracket, the best of things weren't always immediately on hand. If the wine was warm, the wine was warm, it wasn't undrinkable. Such was life, no tragedy there.

"Tripp's here, we need the good beer on hand," Rourke said, closing the fridge and popping open two bottles. "It's party time. I've invited the whole posse."

"Your boy posse?"

Mmm, his boy posse included Zairn. If he was coming, he might have mentioned it to her on the phone, except there were a couple of problems with that. First, Zairn wasn't averse to surprising her. She really had to return the favor somehow. And second, staying on point, she hadn't spoken to her guy since she woke up. Those conversations could be a little fuzzy.

When he called that early, he woke her, it was the best time to finagle out her secrets. Especially when she was naked and he turned on his own brand of seduction. She'd like to say that after a year and a half, it wasn't as effective as it used to be. But it was. Very was. Damn, why did he have to be so good at it?

"Nah, just hookers and drug dealers," Rourke said. "My boy posse's busy switching their lives to autopilot. We've got a marathon coming up."

Tripp swung into the stool behind Roxie's. "What happens at the bachelor party…"

She twisted to tip her chin his way. "You're going to the bachelor party?"

"Was thinking about it. You didn't get an invite?"

"Buddy, if I wanted to be there, I'd be there. To that man, I am the party."

"Yet you're over here flirting with me," Rourke said, flashing her a wink as he reached past her to hand a bottle to Tripp. "Admit it, you were a little impressed, Kyst."

"That you can access any piece of tech? Try being the guy who can access any woman's panties. My guy can charm his way in anywhere."

"I would prove my ability to do the same…" Rourke flopped an arm around Roux. "But the little woman gets jealous when I talk to other women. She's probably jealous right now."

"Talk. Talk away," Roux said, giving him a push, though he rebounded to rest against her again, his arm never leaving its perch. "Touch. Screw. I don't care." Another feeble push. "Just do it on vacation, far away from me."

"'Cause it breaks her heart to witness it. We don't like to talk about how she struggles to satisfy me."

"Oh, I'm sorry, are you the guy who lays on top of me at night? Most of the time I don't even know you're present. I'm too busy getting myself there, picturing hot guys, really any guy—any other guy." Crossing her legs slowly, Roux licked her lips while looking past her to Tripp behind. "You look like you'd be a lot of fun, Little Breckenridge."

"Not so little, so I've heard." Rourke squeezed his wife to sway with her. "You keep him busy, I'll get the wallet."

"Hey, you don't want to joke about that," Roxie said. "This scrounging Breckenridge will move in and eat you out of house and home, him and his cronies."

"Don't worry, Rox Out." Tripp's arm came around her shoulders from behind. "They don't live in a nightclub like you, I'm not going anywhere."

"Oh, please, please go," she said through her smile.

Tripp kissed the back of her head.

Roux posed a question. "Why isn't Zairn with you?"

"First bachelor party is in New York." Rourke wasn't the one Roux had been talking to. "Guy's got to prepare."

"Is this the Gramercy thing?" Roux asked, completely glossing over her husband's words. "Still? Is Kinloch there?"

"Not yet. He's traveling to New York for the—I don't know, Kinloch says Gramercy's nothing to do with him anymore."

"I guess that's true…" Roux sipped her wine. "He sold the company to extricate himself from it, he can't really show up in the boardroom now and start throwing down rules and ultimatums. The time for that has passed."

She inhaled through her nose. "Except the legacy boys might listen more to him than they do the new management team."

Rourke leaned in to rest his lips on his wife's hair. "I told you all this in New York."

"I wasn't listening. I never listen to you, Hotshot, haven't you figured that out yet? Anyway, during that particular period, a younger man had my attention."

A much younger man… if she was talking about Zay-Jay. With Roux and Rourke, their meaning wasn't always clear.

"Kintyre's gone for that kid, man, I don't know if we'll ever get him back." Straightening, Rourke glanced around. "Got no business brains in the room, who the hell am I supposed to talk to?"

"I don't remember being invited to your week of bachelorette parties, Rox," Roux said. "Should I be offended?"

"We're doing LA, the night before the wedding," she said. "Nothing crazy. Every other day of my life is crazy, this one will be just the girls. No raucous, just us."

"We'll have strippers though, right?"

"Oh, yeah, for sure, we'll have strippers, that goes without saying."

"Might have to swing by myself…" Rourke's arm went around Roux again. It wasn't an embrace exactly. It was, but the woman was also his leaning post. "Join the party."

"Male strippers, Hotshot."

"Hey, if he wants to come shake his ass and take his clothes off, don't break his spirit."

"I live for breaking his spirit." Without shame, Roux's shoulders moved in a partial strut. "I'm getting really good at it."

Rourke kissed her head. "You'll never take me alive."

"That's the point, sweetheart. Imagine what I'll do with all your money."

"Too bad for you I'm leaving it to all my mistresses." Rourke quickly laid faux contrition on her. "Is it too painful for me to say that, Rox?"

Though her lips curled, she just shook her head.

"He just likes to pretend he's popular. It's all an

act. Ignore him."

"I do as often as possible," Roxie said in solidarity with her friend. "I don't know how you live with him?"

"It's a big house. I see him as little as possible. Soon as he goes limp, I am outta there."

"You want to grill tonight?" Rourke asked without missing a beat. Roux wasn't the only subject jumper. "We should throw on the grill. Keep things low-key."

"Since when do you want low-key anything?"

"Since I have a week of bachelor parties coming up. Geez, pay attention, thank God you're pretty."

Everyone got up and moved toward the patio by the pool.

"How long is it until the big day?" Roux asked at her side. "Less than two weeks, right?"

"Ten days from tomorrow."

"Great, that's plenty of time to tear up the town. We should do it. Have a string of parties like them."

"Jane won't want to leave the baby."

"Mommy and Daddy will have to figure out how to do it themselves eventually. Time to take off the training wheels."

Mm, yeah, maybe she should talk to Jane about that. As much as Nanny Jane loved to help, she may not notice if Mommy and Daddy might rather be alone.

"Have your parties," Rourke said. "You can trail around after us though, you're not partying in our clubs the same night."

Though Roux sucked in air, Roxie got there first. "You keep your clubs. I have a global array of them to choose from."

"Oh my God, that's right!" Roux gasped as both women sat at the glass patio table. "They can have America, we've got the whole damn world to choose from!"

"We do."

"We should do Europe. I know a guy in London. Rourke sent him away, thinking it would slow me down. Ha, yeah, right. We should go to London." Roux leaned sideways to stage whisper. "This guy wants in my pants and doesn't know I'm married."

London would be the last place Jane would want to party. Beyond that, Knox wouldn't have it. Unless they agreed to take an army or something.

"He will by the morning." Rourke opened the grill. "I'll send out a companywide memo. Your pants belong to me, Babycakes. Can't have the masses messing with the missus, I won't be raising your little illegitimate monsters. Never forget I can tap into any camera in the world. Any camera."

Roux shrugged. "Watch if you want, honey, maybe I'll take Franco and Guillermo at the same time, get them drunk and take advantage."

"I'll fire them the next day."

"Why would I care about their jobs?" Roux asked. "I'm only looking to get laid. I have your green for everything else."

Snatching up a spatula, Rourke shook it at Roux. "I'm taking away your credit card."

"You do that. I don't use *my* credit card, I use *your* credit card."

"What's his is yours."

"Exactly," Roux said.

The women's glasses touched in a silent toast to sisterhood.

FIVE

"DO I SPEAK before I think?" Roxie asked, phone on the pillow next to her face.

"I don't know, I'll have to think about that."

"Ha, ha," she said without intonation. "Casanova—"

"I'm more worried about acting before you think. Rourke got you in." The tablet. "Have you checked it out?"

"Not yet," she said, relaxing onto her back, staring at the ceiling through the darkness. "But I will, don't think I won't. We ended up drinking on the patio for a while." Until she'd come up to bed, but she had no idea of the time. Hmm, the background of the call was oddly quiet. "Are you at the club?"

"I'm upstairs."

That meant in their place, which was almost concerning. "Why? Is it that late?"

"I missed you. I've got too used to having you on the couch beside me. Gets cold when you're gone."

That was so a line, his swaggering tone betrayed that. Yet, still, she fell for it. She'd given herself over to him long ago, no point resisting it now.

"And you were waiting for me to call? Aww…" Sometimes she understood why her friends swooned. "Baby, that's so sweet."

His humor grew with his smile. "Then why does it sound like you're mocking me?"

She laughed. "I may not get Zairn Lomond: The Legend as he's known across the world, but I get my legend here, where it matters. I'm not mocking you…" In fact, her own heart hurt right then. "I've never been one of those women to believe in…"

"Happily ever after?"

"Not just that, I… With every guy before you there was work, not work, more like… obligation. Not in a bad way, just, you know, what I should or shouldn't say, tasks or events I took on because I should not because I wanted to… My whole life, I never realized that…"

What was she trying to say?

"Love was easy?"

Perfect. See? She didn't need to know because he knew for her.

"Love is easy…" Rolling onto her side again, she tucked her hands beneath her cheek. "Even almost three thousand miles away, it feels like you're right here with me." Not physically, of course. If that were true, given her mood, there would be less talking, less clean talking anyway. "I always feel you with me. You're a part of me."

"Wow, you have been on the wine tonight," he said as she tipped up the screen to see his smile again. "You only get like this on grapes."

"Maybe I miss you too." Truth was, she always missed him, any time they weren't in the same room, any time they weren't touching. "Is that okay?"

"That's okay, Lo. Inevitable. Required."

"Do you think Roux and Rourke will ever have

kids?"

"I don't know." No matter how left field her questions, he answered them. Secrets didn't exist between them. Man, she had matured. "Never given it much thought. That kid would need a lot of therapy."

Rourke could afford it.

"People are getting so grown up," she said. "When did that happen? I'm married. Married! Jane is getting married, though she doesn't know it yet. Roux's married. Lilya's having babies. It happens so quickly. One day you're partying until you can't stand up, then the next you're saying vows and peeing on sticks."

The brief silence came with a slight frown on his brows.

"Are you peeing on sticks?"

"Mmm, naughty Casanova…" She snickered. "I didn't know that was your thing."

"Roxanna—"

"I know. I know. No peeing on sticks without you. Sequoia is peeing on sticks; I'm not peeing on sticks. Do you want me to pee on sticks?" Her head rose a little from the pillow. "Are you ready for—"

"I'm ready when you're ready, Lo, you know that."

"You're a guy, you have a million years."

"Give or take a millennium, thanks for the vote of confidence."

"You're the kind of guy that even long after your brain is dead, your cock will still work."

"Not sure hospitals check for that."

"They better. That's dangerous for a guy like you." No, hey, new perspective. "Dangerous for me! I don't want random kids coming out of the woodwork claiming a slice of the pie."

"You're getting off topic again."

Man, she wanted to feel the warmth of his chest

beneath her cheek, to feel the pulse of his heart. To say missing him wasn't enough. Like in so many areas of their relationship, the language just didn't exist to express the depth of truth between them.

"Does it ever scare you?"

"We talked about the wedding—"

"Not the wedding." Though the wedding's proximity was probably the cause of her nostalgia. "How close we came to losing us."

"You really have been hitting the bottle. We've talked about this. I would never let that happen, not then, not now."

"Sometimes I hate myself for it. The cues I missed. The way I treated you, being so glib—"

"You didn't know this was this then."

"How did you know and I didn't?"

Still that really pissed her off.

"Experience, Lo. Shit, you had me almost from the get-go. I'm not the kind of guy who feels this way. Women… they've never been in short supply, but you… Roxanna…"

"If you'd pushed too much, I would've run away."

"You did run away," he said. "I don't think about those days, not in terms of regrets. Everything we went through brought us here. Right here, baby. Isn't this where you want to be?"

She sighed. "I'd rather you be under me right here."

"I can get on a plane, but—"

"I know. It would be tomorrow by the time you got here."

Not tomorrow but later that day, they had to be in the early morning hours, somewhere in that ballpark. After sleep, that was better, he wouldn't get there until after she was up. Not better but… Oh, her brain hurt.

For a few seconds, maybe a minute, might've been two, they just existed together. In peace. In quiet. As they would if they were alone in the same bed.

"What are you going to do about Crosby?" he asked, his voice a little huskier than before.

He'd be tired. He should be, it was a long day for him, longer than hers. In the name of love and care, she should send him to bed… just one more minute.

"Has he been in touch?" Maybe there was something he hadn't told her… yet. No secrets, no lies didn't mean no suspense. "Is he bothering Salad?"

"If he was bothering Salad, I would've told you. I didn't tell anyone else about this."

"Because you think I'll get into trouble?"

"Babe—"

"You're right," she said.

"It's a symbiotic relationship."

"I know that but this time it—it's different this time."

"Why is it different?"

"There's a world out there. A whole bunch of people. They gobble this stuff up—"

"We need those people, Lo. You love those people. You play to this shit, you've never had a problem with it. I always give you the lead with media strategy."

Because she wasn't a defer type of woman. Some of their early memories adopted a different hue, knowing now what she didn't then.

"It's different," she murmured. "I love you more than I love those people. This is your wedding too, you should be happy. This should be one of the happiest times in your life. You should be allowed to enjoy it just the same as everyone else without fielding wild, ridiculous accusations."

"I got the girl; I don't need anything else."

"I feel sorry for her."

Not "the girl" because she was the girl he got. The woman in the story, the fake mistress, she was the one who deserved their sympathy.

"I know. Do you really think this will matter? Shit happens, we deal with it. In the long run, who cares? When we look back at our lives…" He wasn't all that big on looking back when forward was an option. "We'll remember the wedding. We'll remember the love. This will mean squat."

Again, he was right, she took a deep breath.

"People are exploited for… Why do assholes like Whey get away with being the scum of the earth? No one comments on his life and he actually is having an affair." More than one, no doubt. "You're incredible. Smart. Funny. Gorgeous. You're so kindhearted, so generous. You take so many hits—you're a good man, Zairn Lomond. So good. God, it doesn't cover it when—I love you."

Their relationship was solid. She didn't care what people thought about that so long as her and Zairn knew the truth. Which they did. This wasn't about her or them, it was about such an incredible man being so misunderstood.

"What we are is not their business."

Those soft words did so much to bring her peace. "Never."

"Isn't it what you tell your girls? Providing you and I are on the same page, that's all you care about. We're impervious to the bullshit."

"I care about you first, before anything else. What if, with this or something else, they really hurt you and I don't see it. I don't want you to go through anything alone. They're always coming after you. It's a game, I get that, and, you're right, I do enjoy playing it most of the time. I do… but if anything was to hurt you…"

Sometimes she wanted to do more. For all his talents, Zairn wasn't the best at advocating for himself and often (see: always) put others ahead of himself. If anyone should be defending him, it should be his girl. Her missing signals had almost cost them their relationship once and Zairn got hurt. That wouldn't happen again, she wouldn't let it.

In the last year and a half, she'd learned the best way to ensure their intimacy was to give voice to her thoughts. To him. Zairn taught her the importance of communication. Even when she was muddled, only half making sense, she still said the words out loud to him. It always—*always*—made it better, cured her, soothed her… How had she ever survived without him?

"You know me better than anyone else ever has or will, Roxanna."

"But I get distracted sometimes," she said, frustrated at herself, "with the fun of it, the theater. It's hot to have you like that, for us to be in on our own secret, our own truth, for them to get it so wrong. Except I could get caught up in the game and miss that something's tearing you apart."

"You know me, Lo, you won't miss it."

So she liked to think. But they weren't always in the same room, the same state, the same country! Video calling was one thing, and they'd got good at it, but it was no substitute for looking into his eyes and breathing him in.

"I missed it before," she said. "I tell you not to call when these things happen because it pisses me off if you think I've been hurt by a lie. I know it's a lie. You never have to justify these nonsense stories. Since way back when. Don't insult me by assuming I don't know you. Of course I know they're lies."

"I know you do."

"That doesn't mean you shouldn't call if they

hurt you."

"I got the girl, Lo," he said, plain and simple. "I got the girl." And that completed his world? She completed his world. Mmm, ditto. "Am I going to lose the girl?"

Her smile flourished; he knew the answer. "Not a chance, Party Boy, I signed that certificate in permanent ink."

"That's what I thought. So, tell me, why does Crosby's tablet matter? You wanted to check out what he has that's us related? Lies or truth, give it a few days and we'll read about it in the papers."

A whisper of laughter left on her next exhale. "You just don't like it when I brew capers."

"I love whatever you brew, baby," he said. "Especially when Toria's not in the room. Though… I doubt Roux's any safer on that score."

"You'd still bail me out."

"Sure, 'cause I don't want to spend our wedding night alone. What happened the night we got married?"

"I got arrested. You bailed me out."

"Yes, and I will always be around to bail you out whenever, wherever."

"My romantic Scroogey. I thought this whole marriage thing was so you could invoke spousal privilege if you end up in tax court or something."

"Well, that too. What's mine is yours, that includes secrets."

"I'll take them to my grave, Casanova."

"I'll be there waiting for you on the other side."

"You won't die first."

"I won't hang out here without you," he said. "Where's the fun in that?"

"With your cock in retirement…" which they'd previously discussed, "I don't imagine there will be much. Remember what I said about your exchange student."

"We getting to the, 'til death do us part, bit?"

"I can't wait to hear your vows, I'm excited."

"I can't recycle the old ones?"

"No! They're old, I've heard them. I need to hear new vows. Shiny new ones."

Not like he had any trouble with words or the charm. Regardless of the day or the occasion, he always said the right thing.

"Okay, I can do that," he said. "Just let me check the tapes of Kintyre's wedding."

"I was there, Skippy. I heard those vows. They're not shiny new."

"Not his latest wedding, his first one."

Her mouth opened wide in silent shock. "To Julietta?" Affronted, she sat up. "His evil, duplicitous ex? You wouldn't dare!"

He laughed. "Don't worry, I doubt Julietta got an invite to our wedding. She'll never know."

"I'll know. Oh, you'd be in so much trouble…"

"Worth it for the boob shot."

Glancing down, her bare body was on show to the phone that had slipped a little further down the pillow. "Never gets old?"

"Never gets old," he confirmed. "When you coming home, Lo?"

"I have Hatfield tomorrow."

"Blow him off."

"Thank God I heard that last word, or you'd be burning so much money getting married to a skank."

"Ah, damnit, I already married her. Stuck now."

"Roux wants to go to London."

"To get away from Rourke? Not sure that's far enough."

"There's guys over there she wants to sleep with," she said, aware he'd know it was part of the couple's game. "And she thinks it's unfair you're having a series of bachelor parties."

"You party every night, babe."

"Yeah, but not with strippers," she teased.

"I'll come take my clothes off for you any time, Lola Bunny."

Another laugh, and she lay down again, scooping up the phone to hold it above her face.

"Oh my God, can you imagine? Jane would never make it to the altar, she'd have a heart attack and die right there."

"Have as many parties as you want, baby. I love it when you party."

"You love it when I'm happy."

"I do."

"Ten days too early for those words."

"I'm practicing."

"Doesn't it feel stupid to have a series of bachelor parties when you're not even a bachelor anymore?"

"Whose fault is that?"

"Uh, yours. Our marriage wasn't my idea."

"You announced it on *Talk at Sunset*."

"Our engagement, not our actual wedding. You and Ballard brewed that up on your own. I'm not the only caper brewer."

"Ever sorry we did it that way?"

Licking her lips, her joy shone through. "I asked Roux that question about her marriage tonight."

"Shit, I'm glad Rourke did it that way."

"Because it gives us the opportunity to deflect if anyone finds out about our sneaky nuptials?"

"Because it would be a hostage situation, they'd have like a vow-off or something."

Exactly what Roux said.

"What if you look so hot in your tux at the altar,

I need to have you there and then?"

"Baby, if you don't make it back here before that day, I'll be coming up that aisle to you."

"So many things I could do with that statement… Good luck getting through all those layers of tulle, buddy."

"Didn't you have them put in an emergency access?"

Emerg—God, he was hilarious.

"Unfortunately, all my head space for dresses went on making sure they get Jane's right, Casanova. You know, the dress she's never seen let alone worn. Probably the biggest, most important, decision of Jane's life so far."

"And it's in your and Toria's hands. Big gamble."

"Worth it if we get it right."

"That's what Knox says."

The heaviness of his eyes reminded her of the hour.

Rolling onto her side, she propped the phone up on the vacant pillow by hers. "I'm going to close my eyes now," she said. He'd never ring off first, not that night. The only way to get him to rest was to do it herself. "Want to watch me sleep for a while?"

"You know I do."

"Perv," she played. "You're a voyeur."

"You're a provocateur."

"Sex pest."

"Love of my life."

The sincerity of that truth lightened her every atom. Oh, he always won when it came to saying the right thing at the right moment.

"It's rude to call people names, Casanova."

"You started it.

"And I hope it never ends," she said, opening her eyes just for a blink long enough to see his one last time.

"I love you, Scroogey."

"I love you too, Lola. Sleep."

And in the morning, she'd call again, or he would. They may spend time apart, but they were never without each other. He was her everything. Always.

SIX

IF THERE WAS one person in the world who wouldn't expect her to come a-knockin,' it had to be the guy who lived on the other side of the apartment door.

Security loitered over her shoulder, doing their thing, being vigilant. Good job.

Now back in LA, Astrid had offered to do the task for her, but no, she was no coward. If Roxie had to knock, knock, knock all day…

Unless he'd gone out. People did that. She was out, if randoms came knocking on her door—okay, so that wasn't exactly possible these days—

When the door popped from the frame, her posture and expression changed, starlight on.

"Good afternoon, Mr. Crosby… Hmm…" This was no dazzling professional. Weren't reporters supposed to be switched on and ready at all times? Always prepared for the story? She could be a story, right there on his doorstep, and he definitely wasn't ready. "Do you know it's afternoon?" His hair stuck out fifty different ways, his eyes were heavy, skin dull. "Are you ill?"

"I was out late, I—" And then he really took things in. "Why are you—what are you doing here, Miss Kyst?"

Oh, formal, why was he going with that? "You're not going to invite me in?"

In his defense, she rarely invited him in when he came a-knockin' for her.

"I don't have a skyscraper penthouse."

She leaned in. "Neither did I. Do we need a history lesson out here in the hallway? I'm from Regular Land too."

Home was home, even if it wasn't pristine. Jane was the reason their Chicago pad was spotless. She couldn't remember the last time she'd taken initiative herself. Sure, she did chores, that Jane assigned. On her own initiative, she'd only get it wrong anyway.

"Okay. Please, come in."

Keeping hold of the door, he stepped back, sweeping an arm her way. Security ducked around her first, something he hadn't expected judging by his expression.

"It's their thing. You're not vetted. Sorry."

Was she sorry? No one wanted their home to be invaded, but Zairn had his reasons and she'd always trust them. If it made him happy, it made her happy too. Funny that he always felt she was safer when they were together. Yes, that meant more bodies protecting them, but if someone wanted to hurt her, chances were they wanted to hurt Zairn too. His chivalrous self would get between her and danger, of course, what she relied on was Ballard getting between her guy and the baddie first.

Security gave her the nod of admission before clearing the doorway and letting her inside. The apartment wasn't offensive, there was just little to it. She'd seen tidier but didn't fear catching anything.

"You want anything to drink? I have soda and vodka."

"Staples," she said, going to look out the window at the street below before answering him over her shoulder. "No, thank you, I'm good."

"Here to threaten me some more?"

Dipping a hand into her bag, she spun on the spot and produced the tablet. "Missing something?"

"Shit," he said. "I wanted to believe I dropped it somewhere."

"You did. On my couch," she said, leaving the window to put it on the coffee table. "You don't have to worry. Any secrets you have on there are safe."

The tilt of his head and narrowing of his eyes was dubious. "You telling me The Great Zairn Lomond doesn't know someone who'd get through a passcode?"

"He does. The Great Zairn Lomond, which I take as a compliment, not in the snide way you just said it, is in New York."

"He has buddies out here."

"He has buddies everywhere," she said, exaggerating the last word. "Rather than be hostile, you should know he was the one advocating two wrongs don't make a right."

"Roxie—"

"You have your tablet back. Safe. Unviolated."

"I don't get it."

"Whatever you're going to write about us, you'll write it either way. It is funny though…"

"What's funny? That you stole my property?"

"Your affront is funny given you invade people's lives for a living. And no one stole anything, you left your property in my residence. My guy often leaves his love seed inside me, would you accuse me of stealing that too?"

It was so much better to just be her and not

concern herself with giving him sound bites. If she did, so what? Not like she would say anything incriminating… would she?

"That's given voluntarily."

A quip died on her wide mouthed inhale. Yeah, this wouldn't be the best time to joke about consent. Reporter, Roxie, this guy was a reporter. And men could be violated too. Not her guy, when it came to her, but other guys.

"Your property has been returned to you," she said. See, very mature. "Write about this if you want, but please include the reason you came to me in the first place."

In two long strides, he came closer. "You invited me. Entrapped me."

"What is it you have to hide, Mr. Crosby? What are you afraid of?"

"I'm not afraid of anything."

"Good, then you'll have no problem including your own guilt of setting up Anjelica."

"I didn't—"

"Maybe you should take this last forty-eight hours as a lesson. You can write what you want about Zairn and I. You don't need permission and I know you will anyway. But think before you act, Mr. Crosby. This is your business, and I get that you need to make money, but these are people's lives. Real flesh and blood humans, just the same as you. Z and I can tough anything out. I wonder how much protection you've given Anjelica, or did you even think about that?"

"She's safe where she is."

What did that mean? Anjelica was somewhere? Specific? Set up by Crosby or whoever was pulling his strings? Just the notion there was still manipulation going on concerned her. Or was that an overreaction?

"And where is she?"

"You came to set your example," he said. "You have. Great. Are you through?"

He backed toward the door, arm stretching behind him, probably to grope for the handle, only he never got that far.

"You saw the gentlemen who accompanied me here, right? Throwing me out isn't a simple process."

"What is it you want?" he asked. "The interview? I can get you that interview, if you want it. Though you screwed me over last time, is that another lesson? Fool me once—you want to make a fool of me again?"

"How did I make a fool of you?"

"Getting Kesley in there before Julietta."

"Oh," she said, her lips staying in a circle as her eyes went to the side. "You were the catalyst for the Julietta Ines interview. That's right. I forgot."

"Yes. And you slipped Kesley right in there first. Didn't even have the courtesy to tell me."

Okay, uh, that was Zairn. Think Kesley would ever do anything she said? Not a chance… unless it was her playing pretend Zairn to get the woman to dinner. Long story.

Yes, her Casanova could get Kesley Walsh to do anything. That sounded rude, it wasn't rude. They were close, her guy had good relationships with all kinds of people across the world. As Kesley once put it, *"Z is on good terms with everyone. Even those he isn't on good terms with."*

"You give me too much credit," she said.

"You calling me a liar?"

She shrugged. "If that will make you feel better…" He steamed. "Look, every word I say in public is owned or owed to someone."

That switched on his astute stare again. "And you want out?"

She laughed. "Is this how you relate to all people, Mr. Crosby? Every conversation is a lead? A prospective scoop?"

"In this town, it's all about perspective." Which was how she got herself into trouble so often. "And don't judge me, we're not all as lucky to live the high life twenty-four seven. Some of us have bills to pay."

"Invading other people's lives isn't the way to do it. There's plenty you can write about Zairn and I without setting up some innocent patsy. That's who she'll be now, this Anjelica, forever, the 'other' woman. Though we both know she's nothing of the sort."

"You didn't say this much the other day."

"My purpose then was to avoid giving you a quote."

"You're not avoiding it now?"

She sighed. "Why can't we just be human beings?"

"You're a celebrity, Roxie, famous, you belong to the world. This is the life you chose."

"I belong to Zairn and he to me," she said and voila! "There's your quote."

Completely by accident. Job done. Man, she was good.

"What? That's it?" he asked when she headed his way, given the door was behind him. "You slink off out of here?"

"What would you prefer I do? I could press charges."

"Against me? For what?"

"Right now, false imprisonment. If I open my mouth and scream, there'll be a story. One that wouldn't do much for your reputation."

On an incredulous exhale, he relaxed. "You don't get it, do you? You think this is a war, that we're on opposing sides. You don't see it."

"Don't see what?"

"You're Cinderella."

"Cinda-fuckin-rella? Me?"

"We're fascinated, everyone's fascinated. You didn't just enthrall Lomond, you captivated the rest of us too." Hopefully for different reasons. "You've got charisma, yeah, and you're beautiful, you're fucking hot, but that's not it. Not all of it… You're living the fantasy."

Zairn was the fantasy. Crosby was right about perspective. Others may see the money or the lifestyle, the Prince Charming, and it was a helluva view. She got that. Except, for her, it was the man. The one the world didn't know. Her man. Her Casanova. Her Zairn Lomond.

It wasn't often she thought about how her life was blessed. No, truthfully, she thought about that a lot. Things had turned around in a massive way. She hadn't been unhappy in her life pre-Zairn, yet, compared to now…? She'd never been so complete.

Hmm, that might be a good one for the vows.

Jane and Toria reminded her on a regular, regular basis that her guy's yumminess on the yummy scale was high. So did her Delights, and the Crimsettes, and, of course, the Queens. There was an appetite for her life. As she'd been told, numerous times. In her wildest dreams, pre-Z, she wouldn't have expected the media would be interested in her, under any circumstances.

Then there was Casanova.

"I've heard about it…" he said. "The clamor… for the show."

"Don't know what you're talking about." She did. A little. Ish. Okay, she did. "Sounds like you're a smidge obsessed."

"I'm not the only one." When he pounced closer, she recoiled, not backing off, just leaning away. "You are hot."

"Okay, it's creepy when you say that so many times."

"No, I'm talking about your popularity not your looks. You're hot property. Hot off the press."

"Still creepy."

"Not many people get Karryn Keller."

"Why do you care?" she asked. "Do you get a cut for high ratings or something?"

"Is Zairn involved in your show? Word is, he's the holdout."

Illuminating. "Is that what's got you amped? You want the interview before everything else kicks off? It's not about the wedding?"

"It's a lot about the wedding. Your wedding is the cherry on the cake; it's one hell of a launch platform."

"Sorry you didn't think of it first?"

"Oh, I thought about it. Fantasized about it. But I'd never get close, would I? You've got your clique and—"

"Get out of my way."

"Think about it. The boost. You'd get more money. More exposure."

She shook her head. "I'm not buying."

"You lead a charmed life. It's aspirational. Millions would kill to be on your path. Young women all over the world want to do what you did."

"What I did? Fall in love with an incredible man?" Her phone chirped. "If those women fall in love with whoever they fall in love with, they'll be on a path of their own."

She fished around in her purse for the vibrating device.

"Not many of those women will have the chance to fall for a billionaire playboy." He exhaled. "Tell me, what's the biggest thing Zairn's ever given you?"

"A lady shouldn't kiss and tell." Snatching out her phone, she answered and put it to her ear. "Yes, it's charged. Astounding. Miracles do happen. Hold on, I'm with the LA Lurker."

The guy on the other end of the line hadn't even said a word before she let her phone hand fall to her side. LA Lurker wasn't exactly fair. Reeve Crosby didn't lurk like the guy in Chicago, he was more of a bam, in your face kind of lurker.

"Is that him? Zairn?" Crosby asked. "On the phone?"

"I haven't let them speak yet, so I have no idea." Just because it was Zairn's number didn't mean it was him on the line. "What is it you want, Mr. Crosby?"

"Would he ever say no to you? Has he ever said no? What does he do to keep you happy? Why stick by him when all the womanizing stuff comes out? You know it's going to get worse, that as long as you're with him there will always be other women. Do you like it? Do you get to make demands and he delivers to keep you quiet? Shit, the things you must know about him."

Way more than this guy could imagine. None of it related to womanizing.

"Are you going for a record? Most questions in a row. Have you noticed I haven't answered any of them?"

"Give me something, Roxie… I can help."

"You have your quote."

"I want to support you, to champion you, but you don't make it easy."

"We each have our roles to play. Please get out of my way."

"What is it you want?" he asked. "You don't have to be so hostile."

"I'm not the one standing between you and the exit, Mr. Crosby. And you won't begin to know the meaning of hostile until—"

Security invaded Reeve's apartment. Before she'd blinked, one guy had Crosby pinned to the wall and the other plucked her off her feet to rush them out of there.

SEVEN

IN THE BACK of her car, the jolt of it skidding from the curb came almost before the door closed.

"Roxanna."

Oh, his voice, the phone.

She raised it fast. "Aren't you a drama queen, Mr. Lomond? Talk about dramatic exit."

"Lo—"

"I'm okay."

"You won't be when I'm done with you," he said. "Where's your panic button?"

"It's in my purse—I'm fine."

"What the hell were you doing in there alone?"

"I'm alone with people all the time—"

"Damnit, Lola—"

"Hey…" she soothed. "It's okay, Casanova, I wasn't in danger. Crosby was being a prick, not threatening me." What was the best way to calm her guy down? "It's hot that you're worried about me, Scroogey."

"Didn't know I had to prove I would be."

"Aww, is the big, handsome billionaire scared?"

"There's only one thing that scares me," he said, stern, more serious than he ever was when they played. So serious, she sobered. "That's losing you, Roxanna Kyst."

She slid a little lower, cupping the phone closer. "Didn't I tell you? Permanent ink. I'm okay, baby. I'm okay."

"I'm walking out of these negotiations."

"You are not," she said. "I'm okay and you have businessy things to do."

"Nothing is more important than you."

"I'm here, and I'm fine. I have my own businessy things—Hatfield anyway, if he counts as business."

"You ready to do it? If you're not up to it, you can cancel. Tibbs will cancel. Where is Astrid?"

"I told her to stay at the hotel. There are still wedding things to organize. She's good at organizing. And this was my deal. I'm fine to meet Hatfield. Do you think I would let a creep like Reeve Crosby slow me down? Please. That is not the woman you fell in love with."

He sighed. "Being so far away isn't easy. It's harder when you get yourself… involved."

"The only thing I care about is you. If you don't want me to have the meeting, I won't. If this isn't what you want, if you'd rather forget the whole thing, it's whatever you need, Casanova. There are two of us in this relationship, remember? We don't decide things unilaterally." Not big things anyway. "Do you need me to come home?"

Another exhale. "This is always easier for you than it is for me."

"Because you have a chronic fixing complex and take ownership of everyone else's issues."

"I have ownership of yours."

Her broad smile should make its way into her

tone. "Let's be honest, Scroogey, I am your issue. Start and end."

"My crisis event." Exactly. "I have the right to hash this shit out with you. It's hard won, baby, you remember when I said that to you the first time?"

"In Rome. And it's okay, we've hashed Crosby out, he's done with. Next thing on the agenda…"

"Hatfield." They'd hashed him out too. Discussion after discussion crystalized their positions. "He'll have the schedule."

"That's the last piece. We might not have time to sit down with it before the wedding. I don't want us rushed into it."

"Not like you to be nervous."

"Me? Nervous? Pah!" she declared. "I set the rules, remember? And I'll remind Hatfield of them all. There were conditions on this."

"Yeah, and Dunlap has read the final draft. No landmines."

"Won't stop me saying the words out loud to Hatfield. I'll say it as many times as I have to until he gets the picture."

"You? Brevity? That's not your style, Lo."

"No, it is not. I bounce and say what has to be said. You know I'm made of steel. It's one of the things you love about me."

"I love everything about you, babe. I'm too far away to kick his ass, that's all."

"If it needed kicking, I'd have done it myself. I don't take shit from any man."

"Don't need to tell me that." His tension had eased, some. "Do you want me in on the Hatfield meeting?"

"If you want to be or don't trust me to talk for us collectively."

"You know I do."

"Okay, then let me deal with it. We'll call if we need your signature."

"What's wrong with your hand? The ruby too much strain?"

"No, but this is Rouge related, somehow." The intricacies were beyond her. "We'll need your John Hancock."

"How many times do I have to tell you that you're authorized to sign on behalf of Rouge and everything else we own? And this isn't Rouge."

"It's not Lola's Liberty."

No, her hands were clean.

"LoKys."

"Locust? Oh, no, you mean our portmanteau company."

"Your production company."

"Our production company. Helps us make more money off our faces," she played. "We have pretty faces."

"Apparently so. And with LoKys, just like Rouge and Crimson, and everything else we have, your signature's as good as mine."

"Yes, I'm aware of that. But do you think I want to be on the hook if this is a big, fat belly flop?"

"You're the star, Lola Bunny. This is all you and you'll be magnificent. As always."

"It's important to keep the brand relevant."

They'd had the conversation many times, though that never stopped them before.

"Yes," Zairn said, "it is."

"We have to feed the audience."

"We do."

"And what we are is not their business."

A smile warmed his voice. "Never."

"And with Hatfield—"

"There's a difference between what they're

entitled to and what they think they're entitled to."

"Your mantras keep on giving, Casanova."

"Need me to talk about boundaries again?"

She could listen to him talk all day. Didn't matter what he said, just the smooth honey of his voice was enough to keep her warm. Though given she had an appointment, it may not be a good idea to get into what his voice could and couldn't do to her.

"Boundaries are exactly why you should leave Hatfield to me," she said. "You've never been much of a fan."

"Of Hatfield? Yeah, 'cause you used to date."

She scoffed. "We did not used to date, we were friends. Ate a few meals together. Talked."

"Got caught sharing germs, making out."

She laughed. "You made that up in your head and you know it, Casanova. He wishes he could get me, every guy does, haven't you noticed?"

"Mm hmm."

Raising her hand, she admired her ruby. "Good thing you offer me something bigger."

"Mm hmm."

She softened to saucy. "Something better."

"Any time you want it, Lola Bunny."

"Better get that jealousy in check, Casanova. Breathe through it. The pain will get easier in time."

He growled. "No can do, sorry. I'm jealous that the air you breathe gets inside you, exactly where I want to be right now."

"Where you always want to be."

"Mm hmm."

"Where I want you." Every frickin' second. "I'm staying nice and warm and wet for you, always just for you, baby."

"Damn straight, Lola Bunny. Shit, my hands hurt, I need to touch you so bad. It's been too long, baby."

Legs loosening, her fingertips started on her knee, as they rose, her fingers joined them, her palm, all the way to her inner thigh.

"Keep talking, Party Boy."

"Oh, yeah?"

"I'm all alone here… on the warm leather in this big, expensive car. All alone…"

"And if I was there, you wouldn't be on the leather, you'd be on my cock already."

"Mmm…" she purred, parting her thighs further to touch the fabric of her panties. "Would I, baby?"

"Yeah, I'd take that hot, fucking tight little bod and—"

Quiet.

Huh? Shit. Her screen was black, it was dead. Damn her. Oh, well, to be continued.

EIGHT

"GREG HATFIELD, as I live and breathe!" she exclaimed, opening her arms wide as she strode into the suite's living room. "I trust you found everything you need?"

He came to do the Hollywood double kiss. "All I need is you."

"Aww, you're a sweetheart." Somehow Zairn's proclamation of the same also felt more sincere. Of course his was more about love and Hatfield's was all about the money. "Thank you. Should we…"

She gestured at the couch and they sat.

Was this what the First Lady felt like? Shuttling people this way and that. Playing hostess had become second nature. In the club, in the boardroom, integrating into Zairn's life had been so seamless that she almost hadn't noticed it was happening. Now it was just… life.

When he said things belonged to her, he meant it. In fact, he'd laid things directly in her path, or had others do it, which often forced her to act. His life was hers, their symbiosis was—okay, so she wasn't getting into that team building, cult crap.

"Zairn's still in New York?" Hatfield asked.

"Yes, you don't have to worry about him pouncing on us unexpectedly."

That was a joke, it was a joke. Justifying it felt necessary even though Zairn wasn't in the room. He'd never doubt her loyalty but maybe had lingering trauma from her friendship with Hatfield during the documentary.

"You know I remember meeting him the first time," he said, retrieving paperwork and a Dyce device. "Do you remember that day?"

"In Boston, yeah, I remember. The eyelashes." The familiarity of his expression sparked some nostalgia in her too. "That was more than a year ago."

Thinking about it now, she'd known Greg Hatfield almost as long as she'd known Zairn.

"We've come a long way since then," he said. "I never did ask why the Kesley thing pissed him off so much. He hated me from the minute I walked in."

"That was nothing to do with Kesley," she explained. "And everything to do with you and I bonding over eyelashes."

Confusion touched his brow. Maybe he didn't remember Astrid's words that day or he didn't understand why them bonding would piss off Zairn.

"The eyelashes, yeah."

"Though, for future reference, I know from experience that he's not a fan of being set up on dates. Tried it myself and woo, yeah, he wasn't that receptive."

"You set your fiancé up on a date?"

A slow shallow nod followed. "With his ex-girlfriend, yeah."

"Why would you…?" As he trailed off, he looked deeper. "How come you never wrote a book?"

"There's still time," she declared to the ether and

laughed. "The documentary wasn't enough? To be honest, I haven't had a lot of time, what with the ambassador thing and Lola's Liberty—did you hear we're part funding a joint venture with Lighting Darkness and Huddle Hope."

"I had heard about that. I'd love to know more though."

That was kind of his job, always to know more.

"It always fascinates me how much interest there is."

"In your day-to-day life? You're a wonder, Rox. Living the dream."

As Reeve Crosby told her.

"*It's about the man, genius.*" Toria's words were apt, though they were said in a slightly different context. Somehow, she doubted they'd be well received by the director.

"What do we need to get through today?"

"I have the schedule for you," he said, retrieving a folder from his binder to hand it over. "And there's a presentation of the show's artwork, the soundtrack, you'll love it."

Wow, gawking at the paper, all she saw were names and dates, lists of this and that, her life in black and white for the next... however long this took.

"Is everything set up?"

"Just about. We're making a few personnel changes, breaking new people in."

Her eyes rose from the paper to meet his. "I don't know if I like new people. Has Ballard vetted them? Z isn't wild about strangers."

His slight snicker intrigued. "I think you'll be okay with these additions. They're on their way now."

Shock gaped. "Today? I have to meet them today? I have dinner plans."

"You're not an easy person to get face time with,

Rox. I have to make the most of it while I have you. It won't take long. If you really don't want to do it today, we can do it another time, but it has to be soon. Tomorrow? Friday? If I don't make a date with you now, your next opening is probably Christmas."

"Oh, sorry, I have plans for Christmas too."

"Rox—"

"It's fine," she said, taking a breath. "I'll meet them, just, if I don't like them, they don't get over the threshold."

Figuratively, not literally, kind of hard to meet someone if they didn't come in the room. Zairn would just love this, learning she was going to be alone with new people. After her meeting with Reeve, her love's heart rate may not have returned to normal yet. And they were in the suite, alone, with her security on the wrong side of the front door. She could invite security in… Come to think of it, she hadn't seen Stephen that day, he was her main LA guy. Hmm, he'd been pretty scarce of late.

"Zairn approves."

Hatfield's response interrupted her pondering. Did he just say…?

"Zairn a—oh, he approves? Does he? My Zairn? The man I talk to fifty times a day? The only man on planet earth—" and all other planets "—allowed inside my beautiful body? The man who failed to mention new people? Maybe he isn't as fond of being inside me as I thought."

Yes, facetious, what else could she do while silencing an internal growl? Keeping secrets? Keeping secrets? What was her Casanova thinking with so many secrets these days? And, huh, she went on alert. If there were surprises now, what would happen at the wedding? One secret was enough for such a big day. Were there others she wasn't in on? Shame she couldn't corner her guy and fuck the truth out of him.

"Uh… I don't know about that," Greg said. "We, uh, thought you might be happy."

Happy? Now she was suspicious. "I can't even say I'll only be happy if a super-hot, billionaire, fuck machine walks through that door because I already have one of those. Hiding in New York. Hmm. He can't hide forever."

"If you want me to cancel—"

"No, I'm intrigued now," she said with a cleansing breath, correcting her posture and shaking her hair down her back. "So schedule, new people, what else?"

"Your requirements—"

"Those should already be in the contract. Dunlap's looked it over. I've been assured it's all spelled out."

According to her guy, but he wasn't exactly the most forthcoming these days. Maybe she should hide something from him, *surprise* him, see how he liked it.

"He has."

"Rules are: no one in our New York pad, and I have full editing rights. I don't want things twisted around. If I say no, it's a no."

"That was the only way you would sign the deal."

"This is my life, Greg. My life and the lives of people I care about. If something happens and I say out, everything stops, immediately."

"We would never disrespect you or Zairn."

"He would never allow you, or anyone, to disrespect me. This is an odd situation and not one I thought I'd ever… It's important for the brand, and I like people liking the brand. It's what I do to pull my weight 'cause Zairn does most of the heavy lifting with the businessy stuff. He's the bacon bringer."

"What are you talking about? You've carried the

team. Do you have any idea how popular you are? There's a reason the media and fans call you the 'Stream Queen,' we've never seen anything like it."

"That's the problem when you marry for love, Greg. You're left carrying the weight of your mooching partner." This guy was out of practice, Roxie practice, because he didn't relax until she laughed. "I'm kidding, geez. I'm popular because Zairn's popular and I get to ride him every night." When they were in the same state. "I'm the sex proxy for the fans… I talk about it more than he does."

"Okay, which gives me a perfect segue to remind you, we will have two edits."

"Two, yes," she said with a sure single nod. She remembered why the… Okay, she didn't remember. "Why are there two?"

"One goes out on the network and the other is behind a paywall for members on the Crimson site."

"Right, yes," she said. "For my Delights."

"Yes, and anyone else who pays to join the Delights or the Crimsettes."

"I like that we're including our faithful fans, but charging them extra just to see—"

"It's not about the money," he said. "The lawyers were clear this is a requirement. Not to line pockets but to ensure—"

"A mature audience, right." She remembered. "For the naughty bits. Credit card required. That's right. That's right." Crossing her legs toward him, she locked her fingers around her knee to lean in. "Do Z and I have to have sex with the camera crew standing right there or can we set up a tripod?" Hmm… "I suppose there's a joke in there about Z providing his own, but I'm sulking with him right now, so no bueno."

Just since the new people thing. Her lover didn't know she was sulking, but he didn't have to for it to be effective. She'd hold her breath a while and probably be over it by the next time they talked. Especially since he had a habit of talking her in, over, under, out whatever her point was in any call… Though she couldn't deny her own proclivity for tangents. Not that they'd be engaging in that because, right, her phone was dead. Sigh.

"I know you like to play," Hatfield said, "but we have to be careful."

"Relax! I get it. Bad language, sexy talk, maybe the occasional make-out session. We don't have a lot of violence in our lives, right now, I can't make any guarantee about the future. Funny though that people balk more at the sight of nipples than someone getting their head blown off, but, hey, we live in New York, anything could happen." She gasped. "Maybe Toria could fall in love with a mugger or something. Imagine! Have a good day at work, dear! Bring me back a stranger's Rolex!"

He just smirked. "You'll have a roving camera crew follow you, kind of like we did with the documentary. There will be some setups—"

"Unlike the documentary…" Her chin rose until her eyes met the ceiling. "Didn't you say that day in Boston that reality TV wasn't the essence we were going for?"

"Yeah, and your USP is your authenticity. You're the woman's woman."

"The poor woman's woman. Formerly."

It was nice that he still enjoyed her after all this time. "When I say setups, we're not talking straight lies. I mean people popping in or we'll run an event. Your gift is drama."

"Comedy and tragedy, don't they make the world go round?"

"No, that would be sex and money. And you have both."

A knock at the suite door switched their focus.

"Ah, is that our esteemed new people?" she asked. "Producers you said, right?"

"They're just getting started."

"So they're *new* new people. Okay. This should be interesting. I don't mind green… though I'm more used to the paper variety."

The butler entered first.

"I told him just to bring them in when they arrived."

"Sure," she said, standing up in time with Hatfield, straightening her skirt. "And who would—"

"Roxie!"

She knew that voice. Her attention leaped up to the woman rushing toward her. "Bambi, honey!"

The woman grabbed her into a hug and squeezed her tight. The butler was already on his way out, but there was Struan, Bambi's guy, coming toward them.

Okay, so they weren't so *new* new after all.

NINE

"WHAT ARE YOU two lovelies doing here?" she asked when Bambi released her from the hug.

"Rox, these are our new producers."

New in the industry, this particular genre anyway, from what she knew.

"Your our…? Okay, someone fill me in."

Struan explained while everyone found a seat. "Zairn called a while back, asked if we'd be interested in running LoKys for you."

Her joy came in an inhale that ended with a smile. "I knew I liked that guy for a reason."

"He knew we'd been looking for something in that ballpark. In the industry without…"

"Needing to associate with your twin brother?"

Struan accepted the premise. "Close, yeah."

"On the money," Bambi clarified. "This is Roxie. We don't lie to Roxie."

"This is amazing." The production company was needed, what with their vast exposure. It was only right they had some kind of interest in the many eyes willing to watch them. "You're going to run our reality show?"

"We'll be there, keeping things on schedule, keeping an eye on your welfare."

Struan would be good at that given how much time he spent in the gym.

"It's moving too," Bambi said. "We get to travel, be together, run our own lives."

An opportunity Struan had never been afforded in the past.

"We appreciate this chance and will work hard for you, Roxie, I promise."

"Oh, I have no doubt about that…" She waved the concern away with a dismissive hand. "Given your history, it's no question you know how to police drama. And if anyone can make peace enough to stand Roman for more than ten minutes, they have to be good diplomats and have infinite patience. Nothing in mine and Zairn's life will ever tax you more than him…" She tipped her head to the side and back, focused on Struan. "No offense, sweetie."

He just smiled. He probably heard it all the time. Probably? No. She knew for a fact he did. His brother had a reputation. Once upon a time, Struan was tied into that a hundred percent. It was only with love and Bambi that he got his head out his ass and took charge of his life.

"Struan and Bambi represent LoKys," Hatfield said. "Obviously CollCom are our distribution partner, they will get the show out there."

"Are you directing?"

"Technically Greg directs," Bambi said of Hatfield. "We're the police and the prompts. We get things done."

"Ah," she said, though wasn't really sure she followed. The details weren't hugely important, her job was to show up. "This will be a long-term thing though, we need you for everything, not just this. LoKys is a real thing." Now it was, that it had employees. "You will keep managing it?"

"Yeah, your show is the priority. When it's on hiatus, there's a chance of doing something with Logan." Struan's rock star brother. "Then there's the possibility of something in the pipeline for Crimson Isle."

"Oh, that's intriguing."

"We're still working out the details."

And from the way Struan avoided looking right at her, she got the message that Zairn told them not to talk about it. Hmm… interesting.

Tripp sauntered in to join them. "Thought I heard the voice of a beautiful woman."

Struan and Bambi got up to greet him. One got a kiss, the other more of a chest bump than a hug kind of embrace. Shouldn't be hard to deduce who got which.

"You hear my voice all the time," Roxie said. "Am I not a beautiful woman?"

"Zairn taught me how to tune you out," Tripp said, then addressed Struan. "You coming back to New York?"

"For the bachelor party?"

"One of three," Roxie said and stood up. "Why don't you men go catch up somewhere else?"

"Catch up, what—"

"Do a little male bonding." Sweeping her arms toward Hatfield, she shooed him. "You and Stru need to develop a professional understanding."

"We were talking about the bachelor party," Tripp said. "Not work."

"Yeah, but it's unlikely Greg's invited to that party, so don't be rude or I'll tell your mom."

"I'm not invited?" Hatfield asked on rising.

She blinked at him. "Have you received an invite?"

"No, I—"

"Don't worry, it won't be any fun. No party is fun unless I'm there."

"Ha," Tripp said, turning to go back the way he'd come. "She likes to think."

The three men departed, deeper into the suite.

"The party in your pants doesn't count," she called after him. Once they were gone, she spun to Bambi and rushed over to sit at her side. "Good, now we can talk properly."

"Talk… about what?"

"How are things going with Struan?"

"Oh, you know what he's like. He doesn't say much."

"About Roman?"

"He made the right choice, he's never shown any hesitation about us…"

"But?"

"No but, just…" Bambi swallowed. "It's all so much."

"Being with him?"

Excitement burst from her friend. "I love him so much. So, so much. Everything's just… right, you know?" The ease of Bambi's laugh was familiar. "It wasn't so great at first, not him, not Struan, he's amazing, but—"

"The press."

"Yeah, they didn't go easy." Except they had. No two guesses as to why. Thank you, Collier Family… again. "I couldn't stand the things they said about him, and Roman…"

"Lapped it up," Roxie said. "Yeah, I saw his smug face online too many times. Always said he sucked as an actor, but he's got martyr down pat."

"We've been staying at my apartment, *our* apartment," Bambi said. "All the drama's died down and it just works. I love being with him. Who would've thought domestic bliss could be so… blissful. I didn't know that…"

"Love was so easy?" Zairn's words were apt. "It's not all roses; it can be work. Don't take it for granted."

"We are working. Together. We talk. We communicate. It's been… we have Magnus on our case sometimes. I think he still wants Struan to go back."

"With you?"

Bambi shrugged. "Struan said a little space will make a difference. We're building a life together. Now we have LoKys and will be staying in New York… space will be good for us."

She frowned. "What are you not telling me?"

Biting her lip, Bambi took a second to answer. "Sometimes the way he speaks of his brother… Roman took so much of his life from him."

"Like we didn't resent him in the first place. I can understand Struan being kind of tense about it. All the things that were said about him…" Roxie gathered their hands together on Bambi's lap. "Being with you, loving you, liberated Struan. He loves you. His family is still his family. These things go up and down. Family relationships are like that."

"They wouldn't have fallen apart if it wasn't for me. They've been such an intrinsic part of each other's lives."

"Whatever Struan feels toward his brother now is not on you. Just support him. Listen to him. Do whatever Struan needs… except move back to that house. Don't do that. Never do that. Under any circumstances. Brothers don't have to live together to be blood. Does he see Logan every day?"

"No."

"No," Roxie confirmed. "This is Struan's chance to be happy. With you, LoKys, the freedom that gives you… Honestly, honey, he's so lucky to have you. Do you think he'd prefer to be back there? How would he ever have got out if you didn't light the path for him?"

"With the sympathy dying down, Roman's lost his latitude."

"People aren't so forgiving when you're a douchebag."

And the simple smile on her friend's face reminded her of one Hatfield wore not long ago.

"Be serious, Roxie," Bambi said, though there was enjoyment in the words. "Roman might lose his role on *Undercover Ops.*"

"Not your fault, or Struan's. Let Roman take responsibility for Roman, for once. Maybe he'll grow up and get with it." Unlikely. "If he doesn't, let his life fall apart. It's on him, he's a grown up."

Him taking ownership of his own actions wouldn't be something that happened fast. He hadn't managed it yet. Narcissism like Roman's didn't wash out in the shower.

"I can't wait for you to come to New York; you're going to love living there."

"Wasn't too long ago I'd barely been out of Wishbone."

"Now you're an international, cosmopolitan woman. Welcome to the club!"

The guys came trailing through from the other room. "We're going out for food," Tripp said. "You coming?"

"Nothing better to do," Roxie said on a sigh, drawing Bambi to her feet as she rose. "Someone call and find out where Porter is. We can't have him wandering around on his own. And Astrid. We need Astrid too."

Once again, Hatfield was confused. "I thought you had dinner plans."

"I do," Roxie said. "Right now, Tripp just made

them. Weren't you listening?"

"What about the presentation?"

"Presen… Right, there's a presentation. Did I know there was a presentation? There's a presentation, apparently."

"Shit," Tripp said as a troop of people came barreling in. "Are we back in college? I'll need to copy someone's notes."

She didn't recognize any of the new people. Was she supposed to? Maybe. They set up a laptop and temporary screen to blast their presentation.

Bambi met Struan on his way to the couch. They sat together, listening to Hatfield direct the others.

"Like you remember anything except chasing tail at college."

Tripp came to her. "Food."

"Presentation, then food," she said, threading their fingers together. "You know I need you on this and you can't resist a damsel in distress."

"You're a lot of things, Rox Out." He wrapped his hand around the back of her neck to turn her to face the others and murmur above her ear. "You ain't no damsel."

"Sit! Sit!" Hatfield gestured at the loveseat. She dragged Tripp over there to sit down. If she had to endure this, so did he. The lights dimmed and Hatfield flicked the slide to open his arms at the displayed logo. "Welcome to the Roxiverse!"

TEN

ONCE HER BEDROOM door was closed, she headed for the closet. It had been a long day. Somehow, they felt longer when she wasn't coming home to her guy. Before she reached her destination a phone rang.

Hers? Stood to reason, except…

She paused to track the sound and, ah, right there in the dock by the bed. Her phone. Like magic. Astrid was a true gem.

Slipping her feet from her shoes, she went to pick it up. "Casanova," she exhaled his name and sank to sit on the edge of the bed.

"I'm sorry, baby, I've been trying to get away all day."

"Casanova, Casanova, Casanova," another whispered chant. "Skippy. Skippy. Skippy."

And he didn't even have to ask why. "You met our new producers, huh?"

"You don't get away for long enough to call the future bearer of your children, but you get away long enough to find out who she met? Who told you? Tripp?"

"I knew today was the day."

"And you didn't think to tell me?"

"Surprise."

"That's not an infinite get out of jail free card," she said. "You can only use it so many times."

He laughed. "Then what happens?"

"I turn into a pumpkin."

"Meh," he pondered. "I can work with that."

"Casanova—"

"You're not mad, Lola Bunny, or you wouldn't be marrying me in ten days."

"Maybe I'm not. I'll send a ringer."

"I'm not worried. When you're really mad and want to yell at me there's always a charged cellphone nearby. Ever noticed that? Strange, isn't it?"

"You've been working, could be I did call."

An amused half incredulous laugh left his throat. "Do you think Roxanna Kyst, mad, could call Tibbs and let him get away with not handing me the phone? No, baby. You call, I answer, that's how it works."

Boosting back onto the bed, she lay in the middle. "Why aren't you in this bed with me, Casanova?"

"You should've told me to get on a plane."

She pressed the camera button and held the phone up in front of her face. "I spent all day with the show people. Bambi's going to stay with me and Astrid for the next ten days."

"Really?" A view of their bedroom ceiling flickered onto her screen. "What happens in ten days? Remind me."

"Laugh it up. It'll be real funny until you get stood up at the altar, Playboy Extraordinaire. Wouldn't that be newsworthy? The world's most eligible bachelor gets jilted."

"The altar's a bonus round, wife. Do I have to remind you again that we already have the piece of paper with our names on it?"

She loved their secret; Tripp didn't count as "knowing." And it wasn't that she didn't want people to know, no, they could know, that was fine. It was the sheet of paper that got her off. She was married to him. The man she loved belonged to her, and she with him. Who could've predicted that commitment could be so damned sexy.

But that wasn't the only secret Tripp knew.

"Ah, huh, that reminds me, while we're on the subject…" were they? "I have a bone to pick with you. The whole Jane and Knox getting married at our wedding is supposed to stay secret until the last minute."

"Just figuring that out?"

"Me? No, not me. I know why you asked if I'd told Tripp. You wanted to cover for your slip."

"My slip?"

"Someone told Tripp and it wasn't me. Two of your friends knew and only one of mine. That makes the leak twice as likely to have come from your side."

"The leak? To Tripp?"

"Knox and Ballard know, they're your friends. One of them must've told Tripp. Now three of your friends know and I only have one ally. Is that fair?"

"Doesn't Tripp count as yours? That makes us even."

Okay, so she'd claimed him as hers two days ago. Bygones. All in the past. Wasn't everything fluid?

"Possession is nine-tenths of the law," she said. True? Who knew? "Who's known him since he was a pimple-faced brat unable to string two words together in front of girls?"

"Women. I have limits. And that didn't fly with you the other day."

"Today it does. I'm returning ownership."

"Rouge don't accept returns."

"I'm in my cooling off period, you have to," she said. "It's the law."

He snickered, enjoying her in his faithful way. "Where exactly is it the law?"

"In England," she declared, triumphant, because ha! "Which is where I picked up Tripp."

Not that she remembered the salient details of that encounter. Didn't need to with them plastered across the internet and all. She and Tripp met the night of the Logan Lowe dirty dancing incident. A long time ago. Long, long, couldn't be too long, or too far away, a time ago.

"Tripp knows, huh?"

"He has his ways." Which they both knew. She unzipped her dress. "Why am I on the nightstand? Where are you?"

"I'm here."

"Yeah, your voice," she said and sat up in the middle of the bed. "Casanova?"

"What's wrong?" She was scooped up to show his face on the screen. "Lo? Baby?"

"There you are."

Her expression responded to the joy of him. The vision was the sexiest thing she'd ever seen. Still, this view always smacked her between the eyes… and between her legs, in a different way.

"Babe…?"

"Hey, handsome."

"What happened?"

Oh, so serious. "What do you mean what happened?" she asked, slipping off the straps of her dress. "I like looking at you."

All concern, the way he tipped his head to intensify his scrutiny, betrayed he wasn't sure whether to believe her.

"Mm hmm."

"And I'm about to get naked. You'd have to give up your playboy status if you voluntarily missed that. Don't you like looking at me, Scroogey?"

"The more skin the better."

"Good boy." Time for a change of subject. "How are things going with the legacy board?"

"Lo—"

"I'm fine. Talk to me about Gramercy's legacy board."

On an exhale, he sat on their bed. "We're making headway, but it's precarious. One gives, which relies on another doing the same. Everybody's jockeying. Men we thought were—that doesn't matter. Lola, talk to me."

"Did Kinloch arrive?"

"He'll show up, eventually."

"You're never worried about him. He disappears for weeks and months at a time—we should spend more time with him. I want to know him better."

"You're a woman who likes indoor plumbing, remember?"

"Like you're up for roughing it. We could invite him to our island."

"That's too close to the equator for him. I'm still working on getting your agreement to disappear there for a month. Alone. No Kinloch. Just us."

"We can't abandon our responsibilities for…" Oh, he was a picture. Perfect. The only view that could balance her equilibrium. "You make everything better."

"I know. Tell me what was wrong in the first place."

"Nothing is wrong, I just…" Yes, she missed him. Why did that sorrow feel so potent these days? The wedding? "God, honestly, did you ever think, way back at the start, did you ever imagine that we could ever be…? You're everything, Z. My everything."

"You're getting sentimental again. What's

brought this on?”

“Hatfield and I were reminiscing today. About Boston, Sydney… You already knew by then, didn’t you?”

“Mm hmm.”

“I have never loved, or trusted, a man so much in my life. Don’t you ever wonder what…”

“I told you that I would never have let us lose this.”

“Not that, do you ever wonder why we’re so blessed? Why can’t everyone find this?”

“Because it’s rare, Lo. What we have is, it’s like no other relationship I’ve ever had.”

“And you’ve had plenty of them,” she teased to lighten the moment. “I feel kind of stupid.”

“For loving me? Thanks.”

“For all the time and effort I put in with other guys. If I’d known it was supposed to feel like this…” She scoffed. “God, what a waste of time.”

“Those relationships, those guys…” Good clarification because sometimes calling certain guys “relationships” would be a stretch. “They made you who you are, Lo.”

“And you might not have loved me if I wasn’t so practiced.”

“No, I’d have loved you, but maybe you wouldn’t have seen how special this is.”

“Bambi and Struan are doing good, they look great together.”

“Yeah.”

“Roman’s still giving them shit.”

“Unfortunately, there’s not much anyone can do about that. Roman is… Roman.”

“Yeah, and that’s making excuses for him. He’s a big baby.”

“How’s our baby?”

"I think he's seeing someone," she said, her gaze slinking side to side as her eyes narrowed. "In the loosest possible definition of that phrase."

"Do you like her?"

"I haven't met her. Or maybe I have. My head spins with how he goes through women. Is that what you were like?"

"Ten, fifteen years ago, maybe. He's happy, and it's Tripp, he isn't hurting anyone."

"Honesty doesn't erase hurt," she said. "It's the women and their white dresses all over again."

"It exists nowhere but in their heads."

"Yep. Astrid and I are going to the cake place tomorrow. I tried to tempt Tripp into wedding errands a couple of days ago."

"Didn't work?"

"Not his thing. I'll try again tomorrow. Cake's perhaps more appealing."

"You're going to check everything's right?"

"I won't be as particular as Jane, but Knox gave me instructions, I shouldn't fuck it up too much."

"You're more worried about Jane's wedding than ours."

And it didn't sound like that offended him. "Because I got the guy, and you got the girl. Everyone cares about what they care about. If our cake went splat or my dress was an inch or two wrong in either direction, we'd laugh it off or it wouldn't feature. It's one of those things. Who cares if there's too much tuna and not enough steak? What does it matter if the flowers are too bright or arranged with this instead of that. It doesn't change our happiness. Right? Am I right?"

"You're right."

"Jane has been dreaming about this her whole life. She'd never flip out, she may not even say a word, but if it wasn't perfect, she'd feel it for a long time."

Maybe forever. "I won't have that."

"Neither will Knox."

"Exactly! It matters to us that Jane is happy. She does so much for us, for all of us. She's the definition of good people. She deserves this."

"I agree," he said, ever calm. "Knox can do something physical, something tangible for the woman he loves. It's not so easy for the rest of us."

"I'm happy, Casanova."

"I know you're happy. We're happy. Doesn't mean I don't want to go the extra mile for you sometimes."

"The extra mile like arranging for two incredible people I love to be at my back with Roxiverse?"

"Yes."

"The extra mile like loving me so much you couldn't go one more day without being married to me."

"That was a doozy."

"And what do I do for you, huh?" she asked, bringing the phone a little closer. "I once told you I'd never be able to return the favor." And she never had. "How do I please you, baby? How do I go the extra mile for you?"

"You could start by taking that dress off."

Clutching it closer, she gave him an enhanced view of her chest. "The sex stuff must get old for you. You've been having it for a long, long… long time."

"You go the extra mile when you call if I'm not in your bed when you wake up. You go the extra mile when you appear in the office, take me by the hand, and lead me to bed."

"Even in the times I only want to cuddle?"

"Especially those times. You go the extra mile when we're in different parts of Crimson Palace, but you send me a message with a drink that hasn't been mixed to your liking."

"There's something different in the way you do it."

"You go the extra mile when you need me, Lo. When you think about me." He groaned as he inhaled. "You and me, building our life, how you include me in every little thing, even when I'm not there. I need you to need me, Roxanna, though it's never half as much as I need you."

"You like to fix things," she said and licked her lips. "And I like it when you fix things for me."

"Anything. Everything, Lola. You get what you want and you get it right. If anything's not up to par, I need you to tell me. Nothing matters more to me than your happiness. Do you get that? Do you get how much your happiness means to me?"

"You're an overachiever. That's your problem, Lomond. You can't do half measures."

"Not with you, no."

"I won't be able to need you like that when Roxiverse is shooting."

"You can. You will or I'll pull the plug on the whole thing. Anything that gets in the way of us is out."

"The world will see me as moany and demanding…" She fake tossed her hair even though she was lying down. "I mean, I am moany and demanding, but the world doesn't need to know that."

"The world will see me hanging on your every word."

"Uh, you're not the star of this show, Buster. Who's to say I'll even allow you in frame."

His voice dropped an octave. "As long as I'm in your frame, the pleasure'll be all mine."

Her laughter came like a torrent from her throat. "How do you make even that sound sexy? Oh…" She released all of her muscles. "I love you, Casanova."

"You know we're a trademarked brand now?"

And that was hilarious too. "We are?"

"Oh, yeah, the merch money we'll make on this deal alone… We'll build a second Crimson Palace in LA."

"No," she said, shaking her head in the pillow while rolling onto her side. "I don't want there to be any question where our home is."

"Wow, how far you've come."

"If we have two homes, maybe you'll forget to come back to me."

"Never," he said, touching the screen like he wanted to caress her face. "Never, Lola Bunny. You belong to me for life."

"Ditto."

ELEVEN

"NO, BUT IT'S never that easy!"

Ten days went by a lot faster than someone might think. Okay, so technically they were on day nine. The wedding was the next day. Tomorrow! Yes, she was already married to the man, but her girls filling the private pod at Crimson LA didn't know that.

"Toria's right," Rylee said. "We're being pretty smug over here. It's easy to encourage someone to take the jump after our guys already caught us. Before them? No one knows if any guy is for real. Think about how many bullshit relationships and asshole dates we all went through before getting to where we are."

Here were her girls, all together, it was fantastic to see them as a group. It was well beyond time for them to gather. She'd have to make a regular thing of it.

"It's there to see looking back," Merci said. "We didn't know at the time. We didn't know our guys were our forever guys."

Toria may not be as grateful for the gang. Not while in the midst of a how to find love debate.

"Until you took the leap, that's what I'm saying, you have to take the leap."

"I've been with a lot of losers in my time," Toria said, raising her glass before sipping. "And maybe I just don't want to take the leap."

"There is a valid point there," Thea said. "We had to be ready, it had to be… the right time."

"I didn't know I was ready," Roux said. "Hell, I'm still not ready and the guy's wearing my ring."

"Thought you didn't wear rings."

Roux tipped her head and her drink. "No, because I admit my husband's identity to the fewest number of people as possible. And, who knows, I might get a better offer."

"Rourke is a lot of guy to take."

"Oh, ladies, you have no idea."

Laughing, the group enjoyed Roux's tease.

Most of them were in committed relationships, some married, some expecting or breastfeeding. Lilya deserved the break but often got a slightly frantic air. Since birth, she'd been needed to sustain life. Switching that off couldn't be easy.

"Are you missing Zay-Jay?" Jane asked almost like she'd been thinking the same thing.

"I never thought I'd be one of those women," Lilya answered.

"We're all that woman when it comes to our kids," Rylee said, resting a hand on her barely there baby bump. "Even as they grow."

"It's so sweet," Jane swooned. "I can't imagine how you wouldn't miss him, he's so precious."

"We haven't been separated before," Lilya replied, shifting in her seat. "But I know he's safe."

"Because Zach's at the hotel? Is he checking on him?"

"Might be," Roux said. "Until he gets too

drunk."

Lilya accepted the tease with a smile. "Daddy's staying sober tonight."

"You sure about that? Maybe someone should check on Daddy. The guys will be onto the shooters and hookers by now."

"Do you mean strippers?" Mieux asked.

"Depends who hired them," Roux said to the laughter. "If it was Rourke, the whole state will be out of hundred-dollar bills. He doesn't believe in singles."

The guys were enjoying Zairn's apparent last night of freedom at the hotel while the women got Crimson to themselves. Could've gone the other way except her guy knew the music was important to her partying.

"They had a party in New York two days ago," Sway said. "Vegas last night."

"And LA tonight. How many bachelor parties do these guys need?"

"This is Zairn Lomond," Sequoia said, pouring more of the virgin cocktail she shared with Lilya and Rylee. "A lot of broken hearts tonight, a lot of tears across the globe."

"And a lot of relief," Freya said. "Some people thought he'd never settle down."

Jane beamed at her. "He just needed to find the right woman."

Okay, Kesley was sitting right over there. You know, Zairn's ex-girlfriend? The one who'd have jumped at a chance to marry him. Probably still would. Though she seemed cool. Everyone was relaxed. Except Astrid, but that girl didn't know how to chill.

They'd had dinner together, with the moms and more mature women who may not like the sex talk. No, she was no fool, those women knew and enjoyed sex just as well as the rest of them. But some of the matriarchs were related to her girls or their men. With a few drinks, they may have heard things about their children's sexual habits that no parent should ever know. So dinner was a respectable affair, then the group split, and she came to Crimson with her girls.

"You know who'll never settle down?" Rainie said. "Tripp Breckenridge."

"Oh, God, that guy is all kinds of fine."

"He'll settle down," Sequoia said. "It's in the Breckenridge blood."

"When he finds the right woman," Savvy said. "Tripp's a sweetheart."

"I, for one, am sorry I never got the experience," Roux said. "Would be some kind of travesty to take him off the market completely."

"Yeah." Bambi straightened. "Some might say he provides a public service."

More laughter.

"And with Zairn unavailable now, that service is needed more than ever."

"Any second thoughts?" Rylee's narrowed eyes probed. "About walking down the aisle?"

"Oh, please don't scare her," Jane declared. "It's going to be such a wonderful day."

"And you deserve an award for organizing it." Roux raised her glass to toast. "To Jane's wonderfulness… and her secret inner banshee."

Yep, her friend could assert herself when needed. Moreso now that she had the entire Collier clan backing her up. Jane hadn't changed, didn't need to, but she did carry herself a little differently. She got that. She did. Knowing love was a true part of life brought security, the soulmate thing maybe wasn't bullshit after all. Was it confidence? Perhaps Rylee said it better with "smug." Regardless, Jane always found it easier to fight for others than herself. Another reason their secret plan was a good idea.

All reciprocated the toast and drank.

"You'll have trouble when it comes to planning your wedding now, Jane," Merci said. "From what I understand, you didn't get a lot of input from the bride or groom."

"We trust Jane," she declared. "We asked her to plan the most perfect wedding she could, and we have full faith that's exactly what it will be."

"I don't know if I'll get married," Jane said, forcing a smile. "I thought for a minute, but—I don't know."

"Don't talk crazy. Knox is nuts about you. You'll get married."

"We haven't talked about it for—I'm not sure he wants to. He hasn't really wanted to talk about wedding things. He did at first, but…"

"Trust me," Toria stated. "It will happen."

"Wait…" Roux said. "I thought you and Knox got married on Crimson Isle a million years ago."

The misconception was common and hilarious every time, until then anyway. Did Jane really think Knox wouldn't marry her? No, she didn't know he'd ask tomorrow, but had he somehow given Jane the idea they weren't planning forever ever?

"No, that was… The media said so, but we didn't really."

"How long have you and Knox been together now?"

Jane perked up a little. "It's been almost a year since our first kiss."

"Which happened in the hotel Rox is getting married in," Toria said.

"Yes! Day after the wedding will be the first anniversary."

Which was no coincidence.

"You've been through a lot with him."

"We've all been through a lot with our guys."

No one could deny that. Barring Sequoia and her Breckenridge, Roxie and Zairn had been together the longest. Oh, no, sorry, her sister, Sonia, had been with Blayne for… some amount of time. With all its back and forths, she could be forgiven for blocking that relationship from her memory.

Speaking of… "How do you know?" Sonia asked. "How do you know he's your forever guy?"

"You and Blayne fighting again?" Toria asked, used to the tides of Sonia's relationship. "Sometimes fighting is good, it's passion. Ask Rox or Roux."

"If fighting is foreplay, I'm all for it." Roux was quick to straighten a finger from around her glass to point. "But if he's just being an asshole, get rid of him. Life is way too short for that shit."

"You don't know it," Jane said. "You can love them with your whole heart, but all you can do is trust he feels the same."

It wasn't great to hear Jane insecure in her relationship. She always had been, sort of, but with the wedding and the Gramercy legacy board causing way more issues than any of them wanted to deal with, things had been on-ice for everyone. She hadn't seen Zairn in person since leaving New York with Tripp and Sequoia two weeks ago. That hadn't been the plan, not that there had been a specific plan beyond being at the church on time—so to speak.

She never doubted how Zairn felt, or her feelings for him, not since they'd smacked her upside her head. Their kind of security couldn't be taught or bestowed.

"You have to love him more than anything else," Roxie said. "More than anyone else. He has to be like the air you breathe. You can't imagine the world without him, you wouldn't want to be in it if he wasn't at your side. It's right when there is no life without your guy."

"Aww," more than a few of the girls swooned.

"Shut up," she played, fighting to flatten the smile that fought for control of her lips. "Like you people don't feel the same."

"I could live without Rourke," Roux said, nonchalant. "Providing he left the money behind."

"See that's it," Sonia interjected, jolted by some kind of urgency. "Isn't it easier to want forever with a guy worth all that money?"

Various calls of yes and no came out of the women.

"I don't care about the money," Merci said.

"You don't have to, honey. Reid's all about anticipating your needs. He overprovides."

"JD tries that with the kids sometimes."

"Not with you?"

"I'd never let him," Rylee said. "But I have access to everything anyway."

"Yes!" Rainie agreed, maybe a few too many sherries up. "It gets to a point when it's just… there. I don't think about it much."

"Who's single here?" Sonia asked.

Roxie pointed. "Toria, Astrid, Mieux, Sway, Kesley… according to latest intelligence reports anyway."

"Yeah, and none of them had a billionaire fall madly in love with them. Bet if they had, they wouldn't be single right now."

Oh, abandon course. Abort. They may not have had a billionaire fall for them, but one, at least, had been in a relationship with a billionaire who did reject the idea of forever: Kesley.

"Uh…" Bambi raised a flat hand. "Struan isn't a billionaire."

"There you go, see," Rainie said. "He doesn't

have to be rich. Love is love."

"Baer isn't financially rich."

Did that really count? Freya sure was. Rich and then some.

"If you want to dump Blayne's ass, dump it," Toria said. "Come live in New York with us."

Despite her sister's instant jolt of elation, Roxie shook her head. "Oh, God, no, that's a terrible idea."

"Not like you don't have the space."

"I love everything about my life," Roxie said. "Me. I do. Sonia wouldn't do well in this kind of life; she needs a lot of... support."

"You're just through saying the money doesn't matter. If it's just there, why shouldn't I spend it?"

"Money you can spend, sister. Knock yourself out," she said. "It's the rest of the time I'm worried about."

Sonia needed a lot of direction and didn't have much motivation to get up and do... anything. In New York, her sister would be swept up with some group of undesirable friends, and likely a lot of spongers. There was a reason she hadn't set up a trust for her sister. Blayne, and her other friends, might care more about the cash than the kindness. Sonia wouldn't recognize being used.

Zairn taught her that she'd develop a nose for those who were genuine or not, and she had. Sonia wouldn't be so receptive to learning those lessons, she liked to be popular and in demand. Plus, in truth, even if Sonia did dump Blayne's ass now, they'd probably be back together soon enough. And she couldn't live with Blayne long-term, even in a skyscraper. No, the day Blayne moved in to Crimson Palace would be the day she moved out... and she'd be taking Zairn with her.

Sonia was easily led, that was it. Easily led. And would rebel against any kind of sisterly advice, and any

Zairn tried to give too. They'd end up parenting Sonia and they definitely didn't want that to be a part of their life.

TWELVE

"BUT PROMISE BECAUSE it's after midnight," Jane whimpered, slipping off her shoes. "It's your wedding day."

"It is!" Roxie proclaimed to her best friend just inside the latter's bedroom.

"You're getting married today, Rox. Married!"

Restraining the words that wanted to leap from her lips was almost impossible. It wasn't only her wedding day, it was Jane's too. Her friend just didn't know it yet.

She hadn't drunk that much herself; though her tolerance for it these days was astronomical. Too much practice maybe. Jane was over the limit, definitely teetering. Her friend liked hugs and gushed with love on the best of days, with alcohol in her system, Jane's need for love grew.

"I am."

"And Zairn's incredible, amazing, I can't believe you…" And there were the tears. "You found it, Roxie. You found it!"

"I did." Another hug. "You found it too."

Jane sighed as she ebbed from the embrace. "I love Knox so much and I… I can't believe he went back to his mom's tonight."

It was tough to see her friend disappointed. In other circumstances, she'd worry if Knox chose to disappear on a night like this. Not just worry, she'd be pissed, and she'd tell him too. Imbued with so much alcohol, Jane didn't notice Roxie's peace was out of place. She and Knox had proved many times they didn't mind calling the other out in disagreements. Only, this time, she wasn't mad and didn't disagree. Knox was doing the right, though difficult, thing.

What Jane would find out tomorrow, or, rather, later that day, was Knox wasn't at his mom's at all. He could've gone to his mom's, but that was just an excuse to keep Jane at bay.

"Cam's there," she said, stroking Jane's hair. "It means a lot to Thena to have her three boys under the same roof. It happens so rarely."

"Do you think I should go over there?"

"No way!" she teased. "If I'm not getting any, my maid of honor isn't either."

Her job right then was to keep Jane corralled and prevent her joining Knox.

Without the alcohol coursing through her system, Jane would never have the gumption to rock up at the Collier mansion in the middle of the night. Maybe they should've cut her off earlier, but she'd been having such a great time! And, technically, it was Jane's last night of freedom too, her bachelorette party. Another bonus because that was not the kind of thing Jane would agree to if it was solely for her.

If Jane went over to the Collier place, she'd call Knox, and then what would happen? He couldn't refuse to see her without blowing the surprise. If he did see

Jane, on this day, in these small hours, it would ruin the whole rest of the day.

Yes, Jane was a hopeless romantic; wedding traditions meant something to her. The bride couldn't see the groom before the wedding. That was the rule. If they let that happen, even if they could persuade Jane to go through with the ceremony, every time she and Knox hit a bump, she'd blame herself for the superstitious blunder and attribute everything to it.

Nope, wouldn't happen, not on her watch.

"I don't want to have sex with him." Jane sighed. "Oh, I do, I always do, but I just… I love sex. Don't you love sex. Sex with love. Real sex… It's not real until… Love is so wonderful, you know?"

"Yes." Humoring Jane was usually high on the priority list. On their secretly joint wedding day, after all Jane's effort, turning it up to eleven was the absolute least they could do. "Get some sleep, you'll see Knox in the morning."

Jane's grin beamed. "On your wedding day!"

"Yes, on my wedding day."

She ushered Jane over to the bed and helped her friend change before tucking the covers around her. The beauty was already snoozing as she went to her phone in the bedside dock to send a quick text.

> Platinum Suite. Alone. ASAP. X

The moment it went through, she tiptoed out of the room and closed the door without disturbing Jane.

"On your wedding day…" In the living room, Toria was sitting on the couch finishing a glass of wine… or maybe the bottle. "You're getting married today."

"Yes, I am."

"Is she going to kill us for this?"

"What's the worst that happens?" she asked,

going over to lay her hands on the back of the couch facing Toria's. "If she says no and doesn't want to do it, she doesn't have to do it."

"And if she wants to run out of there…?"

She shrugged. "If she wants the three of us to run away together, I'll have Dennis on standby."

"And Zairn…?"

"Will understand. He knows how important my girls are to me."

And it helped that they'd already signed on their dotted line. On the very couch she was touching, as it happened. No waiting. No take backs.

"What if Jane wants you to go ahead and do it anyway? Without her? Would put a damper on the rest of the day."

"Z and I party all the time. If it sucks, it sucks, at least there'll be food and music."

Toria laughed. "Which we know for sure because Jane was in charge of those." The woman didn't know how to let anyone down. "When are they bringing the dresses?"

"In the morning," she said. "They wanted to do it today, but if those dresses were in the building, you know Jane would've wanted to go down and check them." And that would blast apart our plans. "We did a final fitting last week but have a team of seamstresses coming with the gowns. Just in case."

"The cakes?"

"Knox and Jane will do theirs here. Z and I at Crimson, if there's an appetite for it. There's a posse of photographers and videographers coming. They'll be tightly controlled. Super tightly tight."

"Yeah, any kind of -ographers are always easy for you to find. Don't think you have to book them, they just show up."

"It's two of everything, I don't want Jane to feel

like she's taking anything from me and Z."

"You don't care."

"I know I don't care, but this is Jane."

"And she feels guilty for everything. Their marriage license?"

"Knox took care of that. Got her to sign it in with a bunch of paperwork for the houses, the cars, the assets. We considered doing it here, in the morning, but Knox decided against cutting it so fine. I've talked to that man more in the last six months than I probably will for the next six years."

"It's nice that you're partners in crime. You make quite the team."

If they could stop locking horns so often, maybe. "Tell me that tomorrow if this all goes to shit."

"It won't, relax. Jane's wanted to get married since before she was even born. Now she gets to do it standing next to the man she loves and her best friend. You gave her free rein with the wedding. Told her to choose whichever she preferred, she's made all the decisions. This is her dream wedding."

"Yeah, but she's not spending tonight with Knox. You didn't notice how she got this look of worry every time he came up at the club?"

"Guy's frazzled and what's he supposed to do? Jane went on and on at you that you weren't allowed to see Zairn tonight. Can you imagine how she'd react to the wedding news if she'd woken up with Knox? We want this to be perfect for her, right? That means no seeing the groom before the wedding."

"Yes," she said with a certain exhale. "Perfect. It will be perfect, you're right."

"She'll thank us in the long run."

Jane organized everything, the day would go off without a hitch. If they'd read their surprise loving friend correctly anyway.

"Right, Jane's fine, she's sleeping. You can keep an eye on her, can't you? I'm going out."

"Out?" Toria asked. "It's like three in the morning."

"I'm the Crimson Empress, this is early evening for me. I've hardly broken a sweat."

"Oh, yeah? You got plans?"

"Nothing concrete." Tossing back a sly smile, she crept toward the door. "I'll find something to do."

"Something? Or someone? You promised Jane you wouldn't see Zairn tonight."

"And I absolutely promise that I won't." Twirling as she moved, she crossed her heart to Toria then snagged her purse from the table by the door. "Don't wait up!"

Out was maybe a slight misrepresentation. She was going out of the suite she shared with Toria and Jane, but not out of the building. Nope, she was going up.

THIRTEEN

HOW LONG HAD it been since she'd sent the text? Ten minutes? Maybe fifteen? Even if he'd been given the same spiel by Jane about not seeing her, Zairn wouldn't ignore her text. It had been two weeks. Two weeks, for goodness' sake! Her man was probably verging on manic. She had a responsibility to the company, their employees, her friend, to ensure his stability. Stocks crashed when he didn't get enough relief. This wasn't a selfish indulgence, it was a necessity. Selfless. For his health… and hers.

In the Platinum Suite, she set everything up then ducked into the bathroom. He'd be back. Soon. She'd check the tracker on her phone except the thing was downstairs in a dock. Where was the applause? Not her fault it was like three in the morning and the thing was long dead… To send the text, she'd had to plug it in. There should be points, and applause, for that. Okay, so she hadn't needed to go hunting—Astrid set everything up—but it was an improvement on neglecting the duty entirely, was it not?

One she'd made for altruistic reasons… for her man, for his needs, and their love. Yes, she'd come up with this caper all by herself, built it up in her mind, but it hadn't been guaranteed. This was all her. No one else knew.

She couldn't see him, wouldn't. Nope, she'd come up with a plan that complied with all the rules, superstitious ones or not. And, yes, she needed a phone, but it didn't have to be her cellphone. There was a phone in the suite bathroom, she'd used it in the past.

She didn't hear the suite door close. She did hear his footsteps and what sounded like his jacket being tossed aside. That's it, baby, get comfortable.

Picking up the handset, she dialed for an outside line then typed in the only phone number she knew by heart.

He picked up pretty quick. "Feeling nostalgic?"

"That was a different city," she said, her lips curling.

"Same message."

Nice that he could remember a text message from so long ago.

"And, bonus for you, this time I did message you for sex."

"Mm hmm. Jane says we're not to see each other tonight."

"And we won't." She wandered as far as the cord on the phone would let her, before retracing her steps. "I left a present for you on the bar."

"A present, huh?" Mm, his intrigue was enticing. "Thought we'd do those tomorrow."

"It is tomorrow, Casanova. It's our wedding day."

"So I'm told," he said. "What's this for?"

"Put it on."

"Lo—"

"Where's your sense of adventure?" It was a zip of excitement, the heat of possibilities. Damnit, she'd missed him. "We're not allowed to see each other, and we won't. A blindfold is not breaking any rules."

"Shame." His swagger was on form. "I like breaking rules with you."

That's what she wanted to hear. "Have you missed me, Casanova?"

"Rourke and Roux have a rule they always travel together."

"And we have a rule to always come back together." Their lives were far less contained than the other couple's. "Did you tell the guys?"

"Knox did, yeah," Zairn said. "They'll tell their women."

The wheels were in motion.

"Oh, it's out there, no going back now," she said, imagining how Jane might squee. "How did he tell them?"

"He had to come up with something when they found out he wasn't taking Jane to bed tonight."

Funny… though not surprising.

"So it's all about sex, huh?" she teased with mock almost affront. Yeah, she wasn't pulling it off. How could she when filled with excitement at the prospect of being near him again? "They thought nothing of it but wouldn't buy that he wasn't going to get laid when the option was right there?"

"Jane's an attractive woman. I almost didn't believe it either and I know his reasons."

"Yet you mock my attempts to fulfill your desire."

"Not mock," he said. "Didn't expect us to play tonight."

"I'm surprised you're surprised." Talking wasn't enough. "Do you have it on?"

"Yes."

"Don't be messing around, Casanova, I can't break my promise to Jane. You put it on or we're not getting married."

"We are married."

"Hush! Stop saying that where people might hear you."

"Who?" he asked. "I'm alone. Did you bring a guest? Is that what we're doing now? 'Cause I'm sure Dunlap has that mistress woman's number."

"Don't pretend you don't remember her name. You remember everyone's names."

"I make a point of forgetting the names of people you want to sleep with."

"One playmate at a time." Her smile bloomed again. "I'm a one duck bunny."

"You wearing one of these too?"

"I will be," she said, fishing her padded satin blindfold from her purse.

"You are unique, Lola Bunny."

"Stay by the bar. Don't move."

If he went wandering, this would be a different kind of game, the one preteens enjoyed, not the adult-only one she had in mind.

Thank goodness they were alone, what a picture she'd make after hanging up the phone to fumble her way through the suite, following walls and furniture until she walked into a barstool. Ouch, okay, that would leave a bruise.

Her fingertips trusted the back of one stool and went to the next as her other hand hung in midair waiting until... his body, oh, she knew that solid form. Both hands splayed as they slid up his torso.

"How do I know you're my Lola Bunny?"

The vibration of his voice on her palm ran right through her. One hand went higher, seeking flesh to curl around the side of his neck and higher, into his hair above his nape.

"If you don't recognize me in my touch by now," she murmured, pulling him lower. "We're getting a divorce."

"One surefire way to do it."

His breath warmed her lips a second before they met. They'd kissed so many times she'd lost count. The familiarity didn't take away the thrill. Nothing ever would. Their sex life was amazing, no doubting that, but the exhilaration of his kiss was like nothing else that existed anywhere in the universe and it never faded.

His lips retreated just a millimeter. "What made you think of this?"

"People keep telling me it's my last night of freedom. Don't I deserve to go wild?"

The warmth of his silent laugh was as welcome on her skin as his hands. "Yes, you do, baby."

"If I'm free and wild, can I not choose to be free and wild with my best friend…? And maybe a little bit naked?" It wasn't wholly frivolous. "I wanted to be with you," she admitted in a murmur. "I can't be under the same roof as you and not… be with you." If she got too sappy, the blindfolds may not last. She switched it up. "Besides, you haven't hit your Roxie quota this month, Slacker."

He kissed her lips, her cheek, her jaw, skimming a hand into her hair at the side of her head to tip it back. His open mouth trailed down to kiss her carotid, to close and suck in a gentle kiss.

"Don't you dare give me a hickey," she said, joy quaking at the rumble of his low laugh buried against her.

How would she explain that one away in the wedding photographs without revealing their mischief? Who else could've given her the bruise if not the groom? The man she wasn't supposed to see.

"Leaving my mark."

He traced his lips back and forth, drugging her with their gentle caress. Man, he was good at that, good at everything. The angle of his head, the weight of it against her, but not, his kiss there, but not.

Her next exhale was all hormones. Mmm, two weeks was too long. They'd been apart for longer, yet it never got easier.

"Say it again," she whispered. In that suite, on the night of their sort of engagement, she'd asked him the same thing. "Say it here in the dark."

"I love you, Roxanna Kyst."

He never hesitated, damn that was hot. Kissing her again, her head moved as his tracked around to her throat, one of his strong forearms hooked around her lower back to tug her off balance.

"Do I taste good, Casanova?"

His arm jerked her hard against him, scooping her off her feet. "Let's find out."

On instinct, when he bowed, her body braced, grabbing for his stability as he laid them on the floor right there… wherever they were.

He gathered her dress, seeking her lips, almost as if he thought he could distract her from him sliding off her panties. Yeah, there was no hiding that; her body screamed for his indulgence.

Their wedding day…

Unzipping her dress, she laid a hand on her blindfold to keep it in place to take the fabric off over her head.

"Hope you locked the door."

The tip of his tongue circumnavigated her belly button. "We've been caught doing worse."

"I don't care about the sex," she said, parting her legs further, giving his broad shoulders more room. "I care about the date."

Yes, people had walked in on them having sex, or close to it, many times. That was what happened when living a life with so many people in it. And their laissez-faire attitude with employees and friends.

"Relax, Lola," he said, kissing her clit. "I'll make all your troubles fade away."

Fade into him, that's what she would do. He'd take all conscious thought and flush it if he kept doing that thing with his tongue she loved. On a moan, her hips rose, and he seized the advantage to yank her much closer.

Love. It did make sex better. And, for them at least, so had marriage.

The night they'd said their vows, he'd led her from this suite, by the hand, and made an honest woman of her. She wasn't scared or reluctant and, honestly? She didn't have troubles. Yes, money helped, but that wasn't what she meant. It wasn't the cars and skyscrapers that filled her with a sense of peace.

That was her man. Even if they were pauper poor, they'd be okay, because they'd be together. Always. No take backs… that's what he'd told her the night they got married…

FOURTEEN

JUNE LAST YEAR…

HER SCROOGEY WAS grumpy. Maybe not mad, mad, he'd been worried. She'd remind him that there was nothing she couldn't face, except the guy had a right to be traumatized in LA. Her getting arrested again that night sure hadn't helped quell his fears.

But it was for Lilya. For Kintyre. No one should be allowed to mess with their friends indiscriminately.

"I think we should find out." In the LA Platinum Suite, Zairn's arm dropped from Roxie's shoulders to take her hand instead. "And I think we should talk to a lawyer."

"I already talked to Dunlap tonight."

"Not that lawyer," Zairn said. "Come on."

"Do I have to?" Roxie asked, dragging her feet.

"I'm not letting you out of my sight until I'm confident you remember what city you're in." He pointed at Jane. "You stay here. Knox will be back as soon as he can be."

With Z in charge, she didn't have to think exactly, but moving took a lot of effort, too much effort. And, ugh, they were walking out on their friends. Going somewhere. She didn't want to go anywhere, except bed.

"It's the middle of the night and I'm tired," Roxie said on an exhale, hand locked in Zairn's as he carted her out of the hotel suite. "If you want me to apologize thoroughly…" Zairn pressed the elevator call button and she wrapped their joined hands around her body to rest her weight on him. "You better get me to bed soon."

With another guy, she might wonder if there was enough juice in her tank to rev him up. That was the great thing about being with Zairn, about loving him, even tired and jail-weary, he'd still be able to get her in the mood in four seconds flat.

"We have something to do before bed." He tucked her hair behind her ear. "This is nonnegotiable."

"Non…" The elevator opened and he took them inside. "Are we going to an orgy or one of your drug-addled friends' parties? Getting arrested twice in one night might be some kind of record."

In LA? Probably not. But for her it would be on the highlight reel, maybe not a positive highlight, but definitely notable.

"We're going downstairs," he said, watching the floor numbers descend.

"To where?"

"You'll see."

His surprises usually worked out in her favor.

"What happened on your date with Kesley?" she asked.

"You gave me the greenlight setting us up. We had sex in the restaurant restroom, the car, even upstairs in the suite."

"Mwah-ha-ha," she feigned exaggerated

laughter. "And then you woke up with your cock in your fist. You had your fun with that pussy before you met me, now mine's all you get, big boy." Jerking his arm, she tightened the embrace again. "Want to do it in here? We've never had Grand Hotel elevator sex before."

He blinked, his eyes opening on hers. "Think that'll be where Knox draws the line hushing up media for us."

"I don't care if the world sees us having sex. We have great sex. Maybe we could start another channel on the website, do a how-to show. We'll give back to the wider population. You've probably lost count how many orgies you've taken part in. What's one more woman on your cock on film?"

"We leak sex tapes when the brand's on the wane," he said, drawing a fingertip across her hairline and down. "Don't use all our ammo at once."

"We going to get drunk? I'm tired, I might pass out. You can still have sex with me. You have permission."

"Classy."

"Give me a clue where—"

The elevator opened and, man on a mission, Zairn whisked her out and down the corridor lined with hotel rooms. Wherever they were going, it was a random floor in the building. Huh, she hadn't expected that. Where did they—

When Zairn caught a handle to open a door and take her inside, she caught a glimpse of the room number before it closed behind them.

"Casa—"

"Got what you need?" Zairn asked.

Not her. No, when she stepped aside, hand still in his, there was a nervous looking guy seated in the furthest armchair.

"Yes, sir."

"This isn't one of your better ideas," Ballard said, strolling in from the bedroom in the corner.

How did she know what was in there? Because she was no stranger to this place.

"We met in this room," she murmured.

"Yes, we did," Zairn said, leading her over to the couch. Where they'd sat that same fateful night. "You need us to sign something?"

"Yes," the guy bounced to the front of his seat. "I've laid them out. You must sign the affidavit."

"No problem." He kept hold of her hand while he signed, then presented the pen to her. "Your turn."

"My turn to what? What are we..." Words on one of the pages caught her eye. "Marriage certificate. We're getting married?"

"That's what engagements lead to, Little Rox."

At the end of the couch behind Zairn, Ballard approached, not that her gaze left the guy probing her with his eyes.

"Now? What about the wedding? Jane's planning—"

"No one will know about this. It's a confidential marriage license. We sign an affidavit to say we live together. Say the words. Sign and it's done. No witnesses." Except Ballard and the other guy, who Z was ready to identify. "He solemnizes the marriage."

Ah, an official. "So we get married. In secret. Only the four of us know. We continue like we're engaged and go through with the wedding Jane is planning?"

"Yes."

"And this is because I got arrested?"

"This is because I love you and don't want to wait. When shit like this happens—I come too close to losing you too often. This is what I need."

"If I'm going to keep being me and pushing the

boundaries," she said. "I love you Casanova, more than life itself—"

"No but," he cut her off before she could get there. "What else is there to think about?"

"Okay, no but, but…" because she had to be honest. "I suck at keeping secrets."

His expression relaxed, had he really expected her to refuse him?

"That's a chance I'm willing to take."

"I suppose you're relying on my aversion to admitting our relationship publicly."

"You've kept our secrets before."

Slowly, she licked her lips. "Because what we are is not their business."

Married. She should be scared. Run. Cut her losses and—not one atom in her whole body wanted to be anywhere else.

"No, it is not." His fingertips grazed her jaw. "No matter what we get into or where we are, we need to be able to speak for each other. This gives us global rights. We need to do it. No take backs. Us, always. Trust me, Roxanna. Be with me."

Boosting herself up fast, she landed her mouth on his for a quick, hard kiss. "Just tell me where to sign."

The paperwork was straightforward. What a long way she'd come. On the night of *Talk at Sunset*, the first time, Astrid came to her with contracts she wouldn't sign without reading. Now she was signing affidavits after barely a glance because Zairn was the one to put the pen in her hand.

"Would you like to stand?" the officiant asked, rising, prompting them to do the same.

They shuffled out from around the coffee table until she was standing in the same spot she'd been in when Zairn introduced himself after their tiff.

"Do you have rings?"

"Would kinda go against the whole confidential thing if they did," Ballard said, standing at Zairn's shoulder.

"Sure," the officiant said. "Okay. We are here this evening to witness the joining of Zairn Lomond and Roxanna Amelia Kyst in matrimony."

Whoa, boy. "Thank God he got my name right," she quipped. "This could've ended before it began." She explained to the newbie. "He doesn't like it when people get my name wrong."

"What do you think I'm paying him for?" Zairn's fingers threaded between hers. "Quicker we do this, quicker we get to bed."

"Good point. I'm being quiet."

"This contract should not be entered into lightly. It comes with obligations and responsibilities. By entering this marriage, you accept the pledge of forever. Please face each other."

How was she supposed to… They turned and when their eyes met, a grin jumped to her lips. Marriage. Had she ever been afraid of it?

"Do you Zairn agree to take Roxanna as your lawfully wedded wife? To have and to hold from this day forward, for better or worse, richer or poorer, in sickness and in health to love and to cherish as long as you both may live?"

"I do."

And there it was.

"Do you Roxanna agree to take Zairn as your lawfully wedded husband? To have and to hold from this day forward, for better or worse, richer or poorer, in sickness and in health to love and to cherish as long as you both may live?"

"Uh…" Her smile only got wider as she lingered. "I absolutely do."

"No rings so… You have joined now in solemn

matrimony. May you know love and happiness every day of your marriage. Embrace each other and the gravity of the vows you have made today. Pledging yourselves to each other in love and hope, you have the rest of your lives to fulfill the delight you have promised today. Zairn, Roxanna, never take each other for granted. By the power vested in me by the state of California, I now pronounce you husband and wife." He paused. Of course he did. "You may kiss the bride."

Cupping her face, Zairn bowed as if to kiss her but hesitated when she rose on her tiptoes. "Can't get enough of me."

"You wish, Skippy."

Stealing his mouth, she didn't need his permission to take what was rightfully hers.

FIFTEEN

LYING ON THE SUITE floor by the bar was just fine, so long as she could hear his heartbeat everything was good.

"Marrying you was the best day of my life," she said, still blindfolded, which wasn't as odd as it probably should've been.

"You were arrested for B&E that day."

"I choose not to focus on that part, Skippy."

"I've got to admit, you floored me with how quickly you agreed. Where the hell was that woman in Rome?" His fingertips ran over her hair and the blindfold. So soothing, familiar, missed… Shit, if they stayed there much longer, she'd fall asleep. "You keep me guessing, Roxanna."

"You wanted to take me to Paris."

"Offer still stands."

Guys didn't think about these things as often as women. She didn't think anyway.

"Don't you have highlights?" she asked. "After a year and a half with me, you have no favorite moments?"

"Rome."

"The closet or the storm out?"

"The closet."

"Sex on the brain, boy."

"You were the sex initiator," he said. "Fuck, I was so grateful you broke the seal and made the move."

Not something she shied from doing, then and now.

"Would you have done it?" she asked. "Ever? Made a move? Because you had time, a lot of time… and opportunity. And you're not shy, why wouldn't you—"

"I thought you needed time. And I was right. You weren't ready then."

"How do you know I wasn't ready?"

"Because you blew me off the next day."

"Ah, yes, see I have a new insight on that."

She propped her chin on him. No idea why, because it wasn't like she could see him. Habit, perhaps?

His fingers dug into her scalp in a gentle squeeze. "Didn't know you were seeing a therapist."

"I am my own therapist."

"You should pay yourself more."

Rolling over to straddle him, she guided his hands by his wrists to stroke up over her breasts and down to her navel over and over.

"What if you didn't fall in love with me? I didn't know you felt anything for me then."

"You're so switched on—"

"And tone deaf to this, you told me. I like to think I notice now."

"I like to think that too. What with the wedding and all."

Her hips undulated, completely of their own volition. "In Rome, I didn't know. There's nothing wrong with just sex, keeping it casual. I couldn't get all clingy and needy if you were just being a player."

"You're not the clingy, needy type, babe."

"You love that about me."

That was one of the things she adored about their relationship. Even when they were independent, living their own lives, doing their own thing, separated from each other, their love, their need for each other didn't dwindle. No one got insecure or jealous, theirs was a relationship that epitomized mature and secure. Who'd have thunk it? About her? No one.

"Is that what you were worried about? In Rome?" he asked. "That I would dump you?"

"It wasn't until…It wasn't in my frame of reference for us to be anything other than casual. You spend your life jetting around the world and—maybe it was subconscious. My brain just decided to play it cool."

"You were playing it more than cool, Lo. It wasn't all your fault though. I didn't tell you what you meant to me."

"If you'd laid it on thick, I would've run."

"You did run."

His laugh triggered her groan. "Okay, okay."

Now he was just repeating himself. She bowed to plant her mouth on his, though it didn't completely silence his amusement.

"I've got to ask, Paris? Rome? Are you suggesting we do another tour?"

That wasn't exactly what she'd meant, but, hey…

"Why not?" she asked. "We've talked about it before. I want to be with you everywhere. London. Why have we never screwed in London? You have an apartment there for crying out loud!"

"We have an apartment there."

"So why can't we have sex there? Do I need some secret password to screw my husband in the UK? Is there a specific visa I should apply for?"

He hummed, a sure sign of his approval. "We can

screw anywhere you want, Lola."

"We should screw in all the places we visited before, only now we're forever. Now we know we're forever. No one will run. No one will storm out. I mean we'll fight because, yeah, but the real stuff… We'll be on the same page next time around."

"If we do it soon, we'll have Hatfield on our ass."

"Again," she said on a whisper of amusement. "We don't have to go tomorrow. Just say we'll do it someday."

"We can do it today," he said. "Got nowhere else to be. Nothing important on the agenda springs to mind…"

Laugh it up, Skippy. Except…

"I was going to make a jibe about not showing up, but… Thinking about it, I'm supposed to be late, right? I'm in the building. How can I—Toria. Yes. Excellent! She'll take care of that tradition. We're late everywhere when she's in the crowd."

"She's the only one of the three of you not getting married today."

"Meaning… she won't need more time than Jane and me? You've met her, right? Plenty of times you've been waiting for me, you didn't know you were actually waiting for her."

"All the—"

"How is Kesley?"

Many others fell into the not getting married bracket too, hence the jump to Zairn's ex.

"Kes?" he asked. "I don't know. I haven't talked to her. Wasn't she at your thing?"

"Yeah, though I'm not sure inviting her was a good idea."

"Did she embarrass herself? She's not a big drinker but usually holds her liquor."

"It wasn't that, it was…" Slithering lower again,

she tucked her face against his throat. "The girls were talking about love and sex and… She thought she'd get this with you. Once upon a time, you know? You broke her heart then hooked up with me."

"Later, way later. I'd been with other women in the interim." Dayah Lynn came to mind though this wasn't the night to dredge all that up. "She's not hung up on me. Not like you think."

"Men don't always notice these things." Relaxing her head in a roll, her lips just touched his Adam's apple. "Maybe she's not in love with you like when you were together. But when the girls are talking about you finding the right woman before settling down… I don't know it had to occur to her."

"What?"

"That she wasn't your right girl." Tipping higher, she lifted her head enough to rasp her mouth across his jaw. "Why didn't you marry her?"

"You asked me that before."

"She's beautiful." She kissed his chin. "Smart…" Another kiss. "Engaging…"

The next kiss went to the corner of his mouth and he turned his head fast, surprising her with a much deeper, definitely delicious, full French kiss.

His fingers dived into her hair, snagging her blindfold. Grabbing for it fast, she levered up a little to fix it.

"Maybe you should propose to her," he teased.

Blindfold secure again, they were pushing their luck with the novelty and would get in deep trouble if she messed this up.

"I proposed to you," she said, "isn't that enough?"

She sensed his smile. "You didn't propose to me."

"What was *Talk at Sunset?*" Though he wasn't

totally wrong. The question never actually passed her lips… or his. Huh. "Are we the only two people in history who got married without ever discussing it? Where no one asked no one?"

"I like that about us. We're on the same wavelength."

Now they were, hadn't always been that way. This was luck. Her falling into this life, it was sheer unadulterated providence. And she wouldn't take it for granted.

"I want to go to Vegas."

"Could've saved us a fortune if you took me up on that offer the first time it came around."

"If we gallivant around the world again, we need to put Tokyo and Sydney on the list. Next time, Party Boy, we'll spend nine days in that bed the right way." Playing with him was so much fun. "You never did make-out with me that day. Broke my heart."

"Won't happen again. I like making out now I know it leads to other things. Someone taught me that."

"Smart woman." Mm, he tasted good. The texture of his skin enlivened her. "One thing we never got clear, Skippy. Just because you're a one bunny duck doesn't mean the seduction stops. No, you just redirect your compulsion to fornicate onto me. You're still expected to lead me astray on a regular basis."

Even without her eyes, she could feel his energy, his edge. They belonged. In that moment, and every other, together.

"You not getting enough?"

"Sex? No, definitely not, Smirky Pants." No, boy, she didn't need eyes to know. "Shall we go over your record from the last two weeks? Won't be so funny then, huh? Do you know how many times these fingers…" She skimmed them down his shoulder, his bicep. Mmm. His hot, hard—okay, not the point. "Have done your work for you? As much as I love your sexy words, they're even better paired with your touch."

His laugh rumbled through her whole body. "Even better when I can look at you too. How about I make you a deal?"

"Hit me with your best shot, Whizz Negotiator. I'm no easy mark, I'll have you know. I have a lawyer, yep, that's me, I'm a bigshot now." Stroking up and down his arms, her body rubbed on his in instinct. "He's my boyfriend's lawyer too, but I'm sure we have confidentiality…" Huh, actually… rising, she landed both hands on his chest. "Do we have confidentiality?"

"You and me? A hundred percent."

And that was a deliberate misinterpretation. "With Dunlap."

Still hadn't decided if she liked the lawyer. Could go either way on any given day, usually depended on the topic.

"Why? What do you need him lying to me about?"

"Uh…" Her fingernails found their way to his stubble. Yum! "Not me. I'm not lying. You're lying."

"What am I lying about?"

"I don't know, if I knew it wouldn't be confidentiality, would it? I want to know if Dunlap keeps things from me, things you tell him."

"If he does, we'll just fire him."

She tsked. "You'd fire a lawyer for not divulging your personal business to your wife?"

"I'd fire a lawyer if you snapped your fingers and told me to make it happen. There's nothing that I can give that you wouldn't get. It's all you, Lola Bunny."

"Okay, Dunlap can stay."

"There's nothing I'd hide from you. You don't have to ask any lawyer, whatever it is, I'll tell you myself. I run everything by you first. You organize my thoughts in a way no one else ever did or could. Your perspective always helps." Because it was rarely the same as his. Impulse took his thoughts to business and strategy, she saw things from a more personal, intimate, side. "Something comes up and my first thought is—"

"What would Roxie do?" she asked. "My girls do that too. Could be an insult, that's never really been made clear."

"The equivalent of, 'don't do anything I wouldn't do.'"

"Me or you?" she asked. "Either way that doesn't leave much."

He was so relaxed, even in his snicker. "As long as I'm doing it with you, what is there to worry about?"

"You're doing it again," she murmured.

"Doing what?"

"Looking at me like I'm crazy. Geez, man, after a year and a half, I'd think you'd be used to me by now."

"What happened to your blindfold?"

Her lips grazed his. "I don't need to see you to know what's in your eyes."

"That look doesn't mean you're crazy," he said. "It's me astounded that you exist. That your unique, incredible, sexy as hell self chooses to be with me. It's my determination to have you and never let you go."

Always with the lines. Yes, she swooned, but he didn't need to know that.

"Cad," she accused in jest.

His palm slithered up her back to bunch her hair in a fist. Just like that, he flipped her over onto her back. That move. He still got her with it, no matter how many times he pulled it.

"Know how much I love you, Mrs. Lomond?"

"Okay, that's a little hot."

The press of his mouth demanded so much more that her legs parted as her knees rose to his waist. Just as her frisky thoughts swirled their way into carnal, his kiss slowed to a stop.

"I'm going to make you happy."

"You do make me happy." Though she was beginning to resent the satin. "Was this a bad idea? The blindfolds and sex?"

"This was an epic idea. Shit, Roxanna…"

"I needed to be with you too."

"Your happiness is all that matters to me. I promise you, Lo, I'll do whatever it takes to be with you."

"You are with me, and the mushy stuff isn't supposed to come until later."

"The last three days, all I could think is how I'm over it."

"Over what?" The back of her fingers drifted down his cheek. "Baby?"

"The trimmings mean nothing anymore. Every second, always, every moment would be better with you in it. The way you see the world… The way your hand fits so perfectly in mine… Everything is better with you."

"You know what I love?" she asked, still caressing. "The way your arm always stays around me when we're together. How you hold me against you. How you can't help but touch me."

"That's the curse of getting with a playboy, my appetite belongs to you."

"It's not about sex," she said, recognizing his swagger with equal joy. "Though there's nowhere I wouldn't throw down with you, whether we can see or others be watching."

"You're good for the brand."

"Am I good for you, Scroogey? 'Cause that's all I care about."

"Without you, I wouldn't be sane."

"And I wouldn't be happy." Coiling her arms tighter, her shoulders left the floor. "Now kiss me again.

If I don't get out of here soon, we might get caught."

"Least I'd die a happy man."

In a few short hours, they'd stand up and declare their love to the world—like it didn't know already. Beyond that, after the food was gone and the music silenced, they'd be there again, in each other's arms. Hopefully without the blindfolds. Already she coveted that moment. Their last moments apart made her ache for when they'd next be together. Man, was her heart in trouble.

SIXTEEN

THE BRIDAL BREAKFAST was an exercise in discipline. Not so much for her, but for Jane and Toria. Nothing was expected of her except to let it all happen around her. She could sit at the center of the table, drink her champagne, listen to the excitement of her girls... No flies on her. The wheels were already in motion. No running this train off the track. Nope, what would happen would happen...

Did she have time to commandeer her Casanova with a blindfold again? Could they squeeze in a quickie before they cracked out the cosmetics? She was getting a little wriggly. Hmm, maybe she should tie him up this time too. Plenty of uses for that satin she—okay... Flute to the table. Down. Less of the champagne, she still had a secret to keep.

It was fine for Zairn and Knox, they shared the secret. She still had to look Jane in the eye. Sit next to her. Listen and respond without blurting out the words desperate to bubble up from inside her. And guess what? That was so much harder now all her girls had been clued in.

The women around the breakfast table kept nudging and whispering among themselves, grinning at Jane *way* more than was necessary. How was that fair? She wanted to nudge and grin too! Grr, oof, Jane was right there, so containing herself was it.

This was it, the day was finally here. Was it weird she was more excited for Jane than herself? Maybe that would wear off after the truth came out. After the question and acceptance… unless Jane shocked them all with a refusal. Ah, the suspense!

Thankfully her consumed friend was distracted by the day's itinerary. What a beauty. So far, Jane was taking the day seriously, maybe too seriously. They'd shake that out of her after the big reveal. This was her day too.

Tripp came wandering into their breakfast room. He'd been moseying around all morning, in and out of both camps. A fidgety toddler. He came over to stop by his mom.

"You're restless, sweetheart," Alice Breckenridge said, laying a hand on his when it rested on her shoulder.

"Bored," Tripp answered. "This is why I never get up before noon."

Couldn't help that he was designated to have breakfast with a gang of men. Her girls weren't much consolation either since they were married, involved, or off the menu.

"Nothing interesting happens before noon," Toria agreed with him.

"So go back to bed," Roxie said. "No one's stopping you."

They hadn't partied hard last night, but Zairn hadn't said anything about how the bachelor party went down. Hmm, groan, she couldn't exactly ask Tripp how many strippers he took to bed when his mom was right there.

He scanned the table, his expression never flinching from fed up. "You get weird when I single out your girls."

"And you know why that is," Roxie said.

"You can go back to bed alone," Savanna offered. No way his one-day-sister-in-law believed that. "You don't have to take someone with you."

"It's brunch," Merci said. "Who could even pick up a woman at this time?"

"Tripp," the whole table chorused, then laughed.

"I'll go to bed with you," Roux said, biting off a corner of pastry.

Of course, Roux. Who else would be that blatant with his mother still under his palm? God love her for always being ready to play.

"You're married," Tripp said sort of monotone, barely registering they were even talking. "I don't sleep with married women." A little more alight, his eyes went to Roux. "Unless you're separated. Are you separated?"

"We can be," Roux said, wiping her hands on a napkin before fishing her phone from her purse. "I'll just text him real quick."

"No! No, no!" Jane's exclamation startled them all. "No drama on the wedding day. This is the wedding. *The* wedding. It's finally here and everything has to be perfect."

Activity suspended, only eyes moved from one person to another. Mentally calling "not it," they waited for someone to respond to the woman who might flip out at the wrong reaction.

"That's right!" Toria grabbed control. Damn, she loved her friends. "Everyone is here to celebrate love! Roxie and Zairn's love! No one's getting any until they get theirs."

"Wait, whoa, hold on a second," Tripp said. "You're saying I can't get laid today until Zairn gets laid?"

"Sure," Toria said with a shrug. Maybe she'd meant that, maybe she hadn't, but it wasn't her style to project anything but confidence. "No sex for no one."

"Okay, no one told me that was a rule," Tripp said, shifting his stance to something more grounded. "Then, Rox, you've got to do it before the pictures, I am not doing this reception sober." And women were his drug. "This is a wedding, a wedding." He drew out that last word though it wasn't necessary, Jane had already made that clear. "And a goddamn target-rich one too. You've got to help me out."

"I've seen her dress," Sway said, happy to poke at Tripp even in his time of crisis. "Z would need to be a damn safe cracker to find his way through all that tulle."

Tripp shrugged off the concern. "He'll work around it. Any guy worth his salt can. Zairn's a professional."

"Sweetheart," Alice said, raising her chin to look up at him. "All of your brothers are here. All of them. Can't you amuse yourself with them?"

"I know they're your sons and you love them, they're just not that interesting."

Might be something to do with their lack of boobs and adoring smiles. His brothers knew better than to fall for the lines. Huh, she hadn't thought about it. If Zairn had all the Breckenridge Boys at his breakfast, they must be eating in a stadium.

"Buoy will color with you," Savvy said. "He's a sweetheart. And, Alice, he asked if he could sleep over in my room tonight. We were going to watch a movie, something from his pictures, about a fish. Would that be okay, Alice?"

"For Buoy to sleep in your room?" Tripp asked, suddenly animated. "You want to have a sleepover with my five-year-old brother?"

"What's wrong with that?"

Yeah, because Savanna slept over with Tripp's thirty-something-year-old brother all the time. No one objected to that… as far as she knew.

Tripp's single burst of laughter snapped him right out of his funk. "This is a gift. Thank you, Savannah Mayden; I owe you. Morning isn't such a bust after all." He bowed to quickly kiss his mom's head. "I'm going to tell Darroch he's shit out of luck tonight."

Off he went. At least the temporary fix cured his boredom. What a guy.

"Is everyone finished?" Jane asked. "We have a six-minute window to get from here into hair and makeup. And I still have to check the dresses."

"Didn't you do that already?" Toria asked as people pushed away plates and retrieved purses. "Check the dresses were here?"

"I checked at six a.m. and they hadn't arrived yet. They weren't here at seven or eight—"

"You checked?" Toria asked, incredulous. "How many times?"

"Every hour. On the hour." Jane nodded. "And left messages. It's important. Roxie can't get married without a dress."

"To this day, I have no idea how you can get up so early and still be… functional by club time."

Another of Jane's superpowers.

"I need to talk to you two a minute," Roxie said when they were all on their feet, leaving the breakfast table.

"Talk to us?" Jane asked.

Roxie took each of their hands to lead them out of there, through the hotel and into the bridal room. Their staging area was adjacent, but those doors weren't open yet. She'd have to be quick to miss the stampede.

"We making a break for it?" Toria asked.

Jane gasped. "Are you? Oh no, we're leaving."

"We're not leaving. Okay…" Roxie let go of their hands to position them side by side. "Stay there."

Backing away, she turned when almost at the dresser. And out came two red boxes.

With a flourish, she spun around with one presented on either palm.

"Ooo, what are they?" Toria asked, all intrigue.

"Z and I would never have gotten this far without both of you."

"Yeah, because you didn't know who he was twenty minutes ago."

"I only went to the show because of you. I only moved to New York because you took the leap with me. And a million other reasons. You've talked me down so many times and so…" She brought a palm closer to each friend. "These are for you."

Toria accepted hers.

Jane, hands clasped at her chest, shook her head. "I don't need a present. I only found Knox because…"

When Jane's voice broke, she and Toria went on alert.

"Whoa, hey, is that crying voice?" Toria asked, grabbing Jane around to check her eyes. "It's crying voice and not happy crying voice."

"Never mind. Ignore me. Oh, I'm sorry! It's Roxie's wedding day and—"

"Who gives a shit about that?" Toria was in momma bear mode.

"I don't," Roxie said to reiterate her own concern.

The bottom lip wobbled, the eyes teared, and…

Jane just couldn't keep it in. "He doesn't love me anymore!"

Falling against Toria, she was held up by one friend as the other stroked her back.

"Who doesn't love her?" Toria asked. "Because I know she's not talking about Knox."

"Can't be. He's cuckoo for her."

"He's not." Jane pulled back. "Knox doesn't love me."

"He does," Roxie said.

"Did something happen at the bachelor party? I swear to fucking God I will rip his balls off if—"

"No, it didn't," Roxie said. "Nothing like that. Nothing shady or shitty. Knox wouldn't—Z didn't say anything." And it was only Jane's webbed lashes aiming her way that reminded her of the need for misdirection. "On the phone. Z didn't say anything when he called me on the phone. Yep. On the phone."

Good save. She pulled that off... only because Jane's dismay was elsewhere.

Jane wailed. "Do you think he slept with someone else?"

"No! We would never think that—why would he want someone else when he has you? You're a ten. He wouldn't do anything to screw up your relationship. He loves you."

"But he doesn't, I don't think he does anymore. He doesn't."

It broke her heart how in her head Jane could get. Her overthinking, her anxiety, it had been more controlled since Knox. While two of them knew what lay ahead, the most important person, Jane, was making up all kinds of scenarios in her head.

"Why would you think he doesn't love you?" she asked, stroking Jane's hair.

"Last night, he wouldn't... and I called, today, and he..."

"Is this because he didn't screw you last night?"

"No!" Jane said, though maybe not totally convincingly. "He's all distant. Doing that thing guys do, you know, when they're over you. He's over me! I know it! I called him today and he was too busy to talk. He's never busy."

"We're your best friends." Toria clasped Jane's face. "If we thought for a second he was screwing around on you, we'd be over there kicking his ass. Trust us when we say he adores you. He's not over you."

"You don't know," Jane said. "He always listens. He's never busy. He's been weird all week. Last night he didn't want to sleep with me, today he can't talk. What if it's the wedding? What if all this… wedding stuff has shown him he doesn't want to get married? He doesn't want to settle down. And he doesn't have to. He's so gorgeous and sweet and—he could have any woman he wants."

"Yeah, he could, and he picked you. Just like you picked him."

"What if he never wants to get married? What if he asks me to choose?"

"Choose what?"

"Marriage or him. Maybe he doesn't want it. Maybe he thought he did and now he's seen all this activity—"

"That's a lot of maybes, honey."

"It's been all about the wedding, that's not that I—I love the wedding stuff, your wedding, I think I… I scared him."

"Because there were magazines or swatches lying around and he's too much of a dude to care about that stuff?"

"Know what he does care about?" Roxie asked, hoping her smile might inspire Jane's. "He cares about you, honey."

"Care doesn't mean love, does it? Doesn't mean forever. I think he did love me—used to love me, thought he loved me—all the bachelor parties… What if he remembers what it was like, before me, when he had fun, and loved his life? His life was better before he met me."

"That's you saying that. Not him. He loves you, honey."

"Why is the wedding stuff freaking him out?" Jane cried. "He's never pulled away like this."

She guided Jane's head close to kiss her temple. "You stay here, I'll go talk to him."

"No! No, no!" Jane grabbed her wrist to halt her. "You can't."

"I won't let you be upset like this…" And maybe it was time to let the secret out, before Jane broke her own heart. "You don't deserve to be unhappy, even for one minute."

"I love him," Jane said. "I don't want to lose him. And not today… but then… What if he dumps me at a wedding?"

"Yeah, then you'd hate them for life," Toria said.

Which wasn't exactly helpful. It was okay for Toria because she knew how this would play out. Toria was aware that there was a proposal in Jane's not too distant future. They just had to pray their dear, sweet friend, didn't panic herself into a stroke.

"That's maybe a little—"

"Come on!" Toria declared, giving both of them a shake. "This is a huge day, for both of you! Roxie's getting married and, Jane, babe, you pulled off the damn near impossible and built a wedding around a woman who'd get married in jeans if she had a choice."

"Be fair. If I'd been left to my own devices, I might've squeezed into a cocktail dress."

"At most and only if it was lying around within reach," Toria said. "And she definitely wouldn't be wearing anything Zairn might want to take off in private tonight."

The things we do for love.

"I'm going to talk to him," Roxie said, going another step though Jane still anchored her. "It will only take a second."

"You can't."

"I can."

"But you—"

"I won't say anything came from you. It'll just be… a quiet chat. Friendly. No pressure."

"But you can't," Jane said, squeezing her. "He's with Zairn."

"So? I'll tell him to make himself scarce, he'll get the hint. If he doesn't, I have no problem shooing him."

Toria laughed. "You just going to rock up on the man you'll marry today and tell him to get lost?"

"Marry today," she said, understanding Jane's objection. "That's it. You don't want me to see Zairn."

"Then I'll go," Toria jumped in. "I'll talk to the asshole."

Okay, that wasn't exactly the best attitude or approach. Toria's tact was even more lacking than hers, and that was saying something, especially when it came to matters of the heart… or the loins.

"No," Jane said, inhaling so deep, her shoulders rose and fell on the exhale. "No, this is Roxie's wedding day." The beauty backed out of Toria's hug and opened a hand. "Give me my present… please."

Right, yes… Roxie handed over the box.

"You don't have to wear them today, or at all, if you don't want to. They're just a token of our appreciation."

"We've got those fancy fingerprint boxes now," Toria said, impressed. "Like yours."

Honestly? She had a zillion of them now, but the novelty endured for her friends, and it was fun to see.

They opened their boxes and gasped almost in

unison.

"Roxie…" Jane exhaled.

Toria rushed to put her box on a side table and immediately started to take the accessory out. "I am wearing this today. I might never take it off, help me."

As her friend swept aside her hair, Roxie fixed the clasp of the choker at the back.

The mirror above captivated one friend while she helped the other friend fasten hers too.

"I told you we'd get you rubies, didn't I?"

"Rubies and diamonds," Toria said, seemingly unable to stop touching it. "I'm never taking it off. Rox!" She spun around to hug her and Jane quickly joined in too. "Thank you!"

No amount of gold and jewels could replace the two women who'd been with her through everything. This was a big day for all of them. Only not all of them knew just how big.

SEVENTEEN

NO CALLS. No texts. No contact.

Those were Jane's rules. She didn't like it. Before that day, she'd been ignorant to her reliance on Zairn's voice, on his words. And, for probably the first time in her entire life, it bugged her that she didn't have her phone. Rather that she didn't have it nearby. It was crazy! Most days her phone was dead or off somewhere on its own, and she never thought anything of it. Any time Zairn needed her, he'd find her. On this particular day, they'd been told that wasn't allowed. Without the prospect of contact, she got antsy.

Was it PTSD? From that call, the one that told her Zairn's number was no longer active. In that closet… upstairs. Shit, was that really a year ago?

"Rox?"

Astrid appeared around the stylist currently working on her hair. A squad of them worked at temporary stations set up for each individual woman, like models at a photo shoot. Her girls, and some others, had their own teams for the essentials.

"Hey, Astrid, honey. You doing okay? You should be getting your hair done."

"Yeah, I..." As was her way, Astrid seemed a little uneasy. "The dresses are here."

"Oh!" She leaped out of the chair, startling the stylist. "Sorry! Oh! I have to..."

Striding off with Astrid at her side, she murmured, "Has she seen them?"

"No, I don't—"

A wail from the adjoining room interrupted, putting the bustling space on momentary pause.

"I guess she has," Roxie mumbled then tossed out an arm. "Carry on, all! Nothing to see here!"

The busy room carried on, dubiously, but she didn't have time to loiter. Rushing back to the bridal suite, Astrid wasn't far behind.

"Honey..." she said, the moment she saw Jane, back to her. "It's okay."

"It's not okay!" Jane threw up her hands. "This is bad! It's awful! I can't—the whole day is ruined!"

She put a gentle arm around her friend. "No, it's not."

"I knew it would be something. I tried, I tried so hard and—this is a huge disaster! I'm sorry, Roxie. I'm so sorry! They've sent the wrong dresses! Look!"

The gowns were still in their garment bags, hanging on a towering rail, but it was obvious what they were looking at, and there were two bridal bags.

"It's okay," Roxie said, twisting around, seeking Toria who... yes, her friend appeared in the doorway to give her the nod. Eek, it was exciting. Too exciting! This was it! The moment! "Someone's here to speak to you."

"Good! Yes! From the dress place? They'll get a piece of my mind. We're not paying for this. Whoever's responsible... How do we fix this? How do we fix this? If they dropped off the wrong thing, maybe... Could they come back? Fix it? We're short a bridesmaid's dress too. It's just an oversight, right? An oversight." Linking their fingers, Roxie guided her friend not to the busy staging room, but a door on the side wall, a door that opened just before they got there. "Why are they in—"

"Blossom…"

His voice on the other side of the half open door quieted Jane.

"Knox?" her friend asked and reached for the door.

Roxie intercepted her hand and, holding both, stopped her behind the door, ensuring it stayed between the couple, hiding each from the other's view.

"Don't touch it, just… listen," Roxie said.

Okay, this was it, Knox better have his speech ready. Damn, she should've grabbed Kleenex.

"Blossom, you are all that is. The most important person. The way I feel about you… I can only feel this with you. No one else ever came close. I have no doubt we're it, that we are each other's match. But it's not enough…" Peeking at Jane's rapt profile, it was difficult to read. For the first time in her damn life. Jane usually wore every nuance of emotion on her face. Why choose mystery now? "It's not enough that I know that. It's not enough that you know or our friends know it. I want the world to understand what we mean to each other. And that means nothing less than forever."

His hand appeared around the door, ring box aloft, and from the height of it, he was definitely on one knee. Go, Knox! He was getting this. Oh, who cared if he felt like an idiot? The details mattered so much to Jane that he took them seriously. And that was why he was her best friend's perfect match. It wasn't about being the same, it was about embracing their differences.

"Forever," Jane whispered, ensnared by the ring.

"This is my grandmother's ring. It's the ring I

rushed out of bed to go get that night you thought I abandoned you. I'm sorry, Blossom. I've never been so sure of anything in my life. I want you, no, I need you to be my wife, Blossom. I need you to say yes so we can start our forever."

"Yes?" Jane murmured like she didn't get it, then her whole body jolted. "Oh my God! Yes! You're proposing! Yes! Yes!"

"Give him your hand," Roxie said when the box disappeared. "No, wait, no contact, I'll do it."

Snatching the ring from Knox's pincered fingers, she slid it onto Jane's hand.

"Why can't we see each other?" Jane's confusion was a picture. "Why doesn't he want to see me?"

"Because the bride doesn't see the groom before the wedding."

"Before the wedding, but I…"

"We're doing it today, Blossom. I can't wait another day."

"Wait another…"

"This is yours too," Roxie said, backing off to present the room as the women rushed through to congratulate her.

Even the stylists and makeup artists were tearing up.

"See you at the altar, Blossom."

The door closed and he was gone, which only creased Jane's brow further.

"I don't get it—"

"They didn't get the order wrong," Toria said, extricating Jane from the hugs that happened to her, she was too dazed to be an active participant. "There are two bridal gowns because there are two brides. "You… and Roxie."

"Me and…" Jane whipped around to check her smile. "We're both getting married? No, I won't take your day from you."

"I want to share this with you." Roxie went to give her another hug, tighter, more secure than anyone else would. "You've done this, all of this. You deserve to embrace this day with me." She leaned back to make eye contact. "Besides, the masses won't get the gushing bride experience with me."

"Oh, but all the people, the crowd and the…"

"I'll take care of the crowd. You be the gushing bride and I'll be the spectacle bride."

Like they were different Barbies.

"This is too… But there are so many things we'll have to change—"

"Nothing. It's all been done."

"Done?"

"Why do you think I hung around in LA so long before today? Why do you think Lilya kept asking for help with Zay-Jay…? Other than the fact that she needed you?"

"You knew." Jane's head snapped side to side as she inspected each of their faces. "You both knew about this?"

"Yes," Toria said on a laugh.

"This isn't because of what I said this morning? You didn't browbeat him into—"

"What do you think Knox just carries the ring around all the time? No. We didn't speak to him this morning."

Jane patted her decolletage. "We'll need a license and—"

"You have a license, you signed it with a bunch of other things."

"I… I have a license?"

"To wed? Yes."

"And the dress—"

"Right there. Exactly the one you chose as your

dream dress in the bridal store. Customized to our means and the fairytales, of course.”

“The cake?”

“On its way.”

“But I… but we…”

“No excuses, everything is under control.”

“But how did you…”

Jane needed to process. And she’d have time for that. Some anyway.

“Let’s get champagne in here and keep it coming,” Roxie called over her shoulder at someone, anyone. “Just breathe, honey. It will all be okay.”

She and Toria settled Jane on the antique-style settee, then sat at either side of her. They hugged and stroked to, hopefully, comfort while wide-eyed, still stunned, Jane fixated on the floor.

“You won’t miss out on anything and don’t have to do this today,” Toria said, giving Jane another squeeze. “There’s no pressure. None. If you don’t want to marry him—”

“I do!” Jane suddenly became alert. “I do want to marry him… I want to marry him… today!”

“Okay,” she spoke slowly. “That’s good. Great.”

“Does Knox know? How do we tell him that—”

“He knows, sweetie. Everything is planned.”

Was Jane listening? Was she breathing? Given what she’d just been hit with, Jane could be forgiven for not absorbing the details.

“How did…” Jane looked at Toria, then at her. “You knew this was happening?”

“We did.”

Jane swallowed. “This is why…”

Toria filled in the silence. “Why he didn’t sleep with you last night?”

“And probably why he was too busy to talk this

morning," Roxie said. "He had to deal with family, and guests, finding out the news. Though it could be he was nervous to say something wrong."

"There's no such thing as a nervous Collier," Jane murmured. Ah, her guy and her best friend were like one. She loved it. "Oh, no, wait! I'm nervous all the time, I can't be a Collier."

"They make exceptions for beauty and brains. And future-heir makers."

"There's no such thing as an unattractive Collier either," Toria said. "Focus on that, baby, and start figuring out what'll be your something blue."

"Are you sure?" Jane bounced around to take both of Roxie's hands. "This is your day. I don't want—"

"This is our day." She cupped Jane's jaw. "I want to do this with you. I need to."

"And Zairn won't be mad?"

She laughed. "No, honey, he wants this too."

If ever there was a prime moment to reveal she and Zairn were already married, it was that one right there. And there it went floating by…

She didn't confess.

Probably never would.

"We're… getting married."

"We're getting married!" she declared and grabbed Jane into a hug.

A lot of moving parts awaited them. There was a good chance something might not click the way it was supposed to. Did she care? Not for herself, but for Jane.

Either way, they'd work it out. Because they had the groom part right… Not that she'd necessarily admit that to Knox's face.

EIGHTEEN

EACH PART OF the getting ready process ran like silk. Jane's anxiety hadn't lessened, not much. Given that her friend was the organizer, she knew exactly what should happen and when. The rest of them just had to turn up and hit their marks.

When the door closed behind the last floofy dress person, she and Jane were left alone in the bridal room. Next to each other. Facing the wraparound mirrors that showcased them on their pedestals.

She didn't say a word. Jane was fixated on herself, on the reflection of her own perfect beauty, like she didn't really believe it. In her defense, she didn't have anything to believe a few short hours ago.

"This is really happening," Jane whispered with no less wonder.

"It's really happening."

Jane grabbed for her stomach. "I think I'm going to be sick."

Picking up the skirt of her dress, Roxie hopped down to go and take her friend's hand.

"You're not going to be sick. Not in that dress. Though, if ever there were a moment, there's enough product in your hair that it won't move an inch."

"I don't know if I can do this."

"Do what?" Roxie asked, exuding only joy and optimism. "The standing up in front of people…" which was always going to be Jane's hangup, "or marrying the wrong man kind of can't do this?"

"He's the right man," Jane said quickly. "I can't believe I ever…"

"Tried to wriggle out of the inevitable relationship between the two of you?"

"What if he changes his mind?"

"You didn't even know this was happening this morning. If he'd got up and decided to call it off, would he have followed through on the proposal?"

"I can't believe he… he didn't want to see me before the wedding."

"Isn't that the rule?"

"Yes!" Jane said on a rapturous laugh. "He doesn't care about anything like that, but for me…"

"He'd do anything for you. Don't you think Toria and I ran the gauntlet with him? Many, many times. If either of us thought he wasn't worthy of you, we'd have nixed this from the start."

"How long have you known? You and Toria? Who else knew?"

"For most of the time, it was me, Z, Knox and Toria. Tripp figured it out or found out at some point, I don't know when or who slipped up."

"The guys?"

"Knox didn't tell them until last night. They couldn't believe he wasn't going to bed with you."

Jane's cheeks pinked. "And his mom? His brothers?"

"I'd be willing to bet Cam heard it first, but you'd

have to ask Knox about the others."

"I'm getting married," Jane said, awestruck, admiring the jewel that fit so perfectly on her hand. "I'm really doing it."

"Yeah, you are. But what Toria said is true too. Don't feel pressured into this today. We can do it later or not at all. If you're not one hundred percent sure—"

"I'm sure," she said. "Now I know Knox wasn't… He really loves me."

"He does."

"Anyway, I would never do that to you and Zairn. This day is about all of us."

"Zairn won't care—" That dismayed Jane. "No, not that he won't care. He wants to do this. Really wants to do this. Your happiness means a lot to him too. He wouldn't want you marrying Knox unless you were sure. He and I can still do the deed whether you do or not. Unless you want to get out of here, in which case, I have a jet on the tarmac ready to go."

On a laugh, Jane used their link to step off the podium and into a hug. A sort of hug. Wasn't easy to get close with all that dress.

"I love you, Roxie."

"And I love you too."

Still holding her, Jane leaned a little back. "Are you sure?"

"Am I sure, what?"

"Knox and I might have crashed your day, but it is your day too. Are you sure you want to go through with it?"

"To marry Zairn? You know, it never occurred to me not to. Weird, right? After that moment, in the CollCom editing booth, when it finally hit me what an idiot I was… Not marrying him never occurred to me."

"You never wanted to get married," Jane said. "You were never against it, but it wasn't… you didn't care about it."

"I still don't. It's not like something I have great reverence for. The institution is… whatever, you know?"

"It's about the man."

Always full of wonder, Jane was a prize no woman would ever top.

"It is," she exhaled with a laugh. Toria had given that speech more than once. "It's Zairn. Married is just a word. But to be joined with him, to throw it out into the world that we belong utterly to each other. Yeah, I'm onboard. That matters." They hugged again. "And it matters to Zairn."

"Which means it matters to you. You care about what he cares about."

"It's *our* life. I want him to be happy."

"It's always easier for them to treat us than it is for us to treat them."

"They like being in control."

"They like spoiling us."

"That too."

"Roxie, will our…"

Jane's hesitation was cause for concern. She couldn't have her friend go through with this unless she was completely sure.

"Honey?" she asked, seeking her gaze and stroking her hair. "What's wrong?"

"Nothing, I—nothing."

"Ask the question, whatever it is."

"Will our…" Jane surrendered. "Will our children be entitled brats?"

"With you as a mother? Not a chance in hell. You think Auntie Roxie and Auntie Toria would ever let that happen? Your children will be the kindest, sweetest… probably most taken advantage of, in the whole schoolyard." Holding her friend's face in two hands, she brought them closer. "Yes, Knox can be overbearing and stroppy at times…" that the same may be said about her was irrelevant. "But he will love you and your children with a ferocious fervor. There's nothing he wouldn't do to make you happy, and I mean that from the bottom of my heart."

"Sometimes I think you don't like him."

"It's a game," Roxie said. "He's the big brother I like to prod at. I secretly love him. We have spent a lot of time talking to each other recently, like a lot, a lot. You deserve an endurance medal for what you tolerate."

"Rox!"

"And, hell, if it all goes wrong, you can always move onto his brother. Pick Cam, not Caspian."

Jane laughed her away. "Roxie!"

"What? No one would ever know with Cam, and I have it on good authority he's the real Collier prize. Though… hmm… he did renounce the trust fund. Maybe he's secretly crazy, like the 'dead' grandmother or inconvenient wife in the attic kind of crazy. Given his life choices, that wouldn't be a leap. We'd have to do a full psychological work-up before making any final decisions… Hmm, but…" she exaggerated. "Would make it easier to get power of attorney over his assets."

"Roxie…" Yeah, sometimes playing was the easiest way to relax Jane. "You're so bad!"

"Not bad, just considering your options. Once upon a time, Cam was a lady killer. I suppose Knox may have done his share of lady killing… Okay, homicidal maniac is not a good look when anyone could be watching."

"Watching?" Jane's panic hit eleven as her eyes darted around the ceiling. "Roxie, we got changed in here."

"Yeah, and with a figure like that, you have nothing to be modest about. And, oh, yeah, your soon-to-be husband controls most every kind of media there is. And we have Roux, who can make Rourke do anything."

Wouldn't be the first time Rourke had gone in a digital back door to erase pictures or videos… or the entire conversation history of certain peoples. Did he help Knox with that whole getting London Guy locked up? She'd ask one of them later when there were a few less bottles of champagne.

"I don't want him seeing me naked."

"Relax, honey, all the cameras are elsewhere today. This body is only eyes on for Knox. After today you'll be a respectable married woman. Faithful. Committed… in numerous senses of the word."

The width of Jane's smile grew as her knees bent in a bounce, and, of course, being Jane, she couldn't help but squee.

"When I woke up this morning, I had no idea… No… I'm getting married today." And the excitement faltered. "My mom was just… I don't think she believes it either."

"Don't worry about her," Roxie said. "Knox spoke to her. And all the seating plans have been amended to get them up front. Everything will be perfect, I promise."

"I'm terrified," Jane admitted, snatching her hands. "All those people out there…"

"Focus on Knox, he'll be out front waiting."

"And my dad… Did someone explain—"

"He's ready and willing to walk you down the aisle."

"Are we going together?"

"I'll go first," Roxie said. "I'm the opening act, you're the headliner."

She'd be the first to admit that even the dress, makeup, and hair didn't transform her into the perfect picture bride. Jane was picture-perfect. Her gorgeous friend had the glow. Something that couldn't be faked, the biological reaction to fulfilling an epic life goal. Shit, it was almost enough to dampen her eyes, but no way was she sitting in that chair another hour to get the makeup fixed.

"People came here to see you," Jane said. "Not me."

"That's where you're wrong. All of our people are out there. The guest list got Knox's approval too. You don't think everyone wants to know more about the woman who conquered Knox Collier?" She made such a vision that containing herself was near impossible. "You are so pretty."

Toria came rushing in, tossing the door closed behind her. "If you two are done chatting it up, we have a crowd of folks and two particularly focused men waiting out here for you. I've got to say, when I said 'crowd' shit, girls, it's like the royal wedding. How the fuck are there so many people in that room? Do we know that many people?"

Well, it wasn't one room, it was several open to each other. That reminder, though, wasn't helpful. Damnit Toria. The prospect of so many people may freak Jane out, but for Toria, it was Christmas. Sometimes the excitement got too much for her friend to hold in.

"Okay, if we're doing this," she said, locking eyes with Jane. "Then we're doing this."

"Is it twenty-three?"

"Twenty-three what?" Toria joined them. "I don't get it."

Without any uncertainty, Jane answered. "We have to be twenty-three minutes late."

"You timed it?" Toria asked.

Wonders never ceased with beautiful Jane. Why were they surprised? Being so specific... talk about forward planning. A lot of thought had gone into this moment. A lifetime of thought. Jane hadn't known the wedding was happening this morning, not hers, though, shit, she'd sure turned up with her ignition on.

"Why twenty-three?"

"It's long enough to fit tradition, but not too long it might be considered rude."

On her wedding day, Jane's precision, and politeness, remained intact. Even being late was planned to a T.

"Oh, honey, I'd kiss you if it wouldn't ruin your makeup."

"No kisses," Toria said, taking each of their hands. "Not until Jane says so. Now let's do this."

NINETEEN

ONE STEP, two steps. This was so much easier with Jane and Toria at her side. Not that she'd ever be without them. Jane's solidarity was important too. This was them, doing this huge life changing thing, together. And Toria wasn't being left behind, their confident friend was more than happy with her life and her freedom.

Married.

Shit, her heart was hopping. The three of them stood alone in the small, private foyer at the head of the aisle. Doors on all four walls, plenty of avenues for escape. Grand Hotel thought of everything.

The sound beyond the double doors up front signaled people. A lot of people. That didn't scare her. He was in there. Her Casanova. Waiting for her. Something he was accustomed to maybe, but definitely not on this scale.

Was he thinking of their secret too? This was pantomime, theater for their egos and fans. They didn't need to do this for them but owed it to… everyone.

Their relationship had been scrutinized and

dissected on almost every platform, in every form of media. They belonged to the people they cared about, and the people who cared about them. And, yes, that included the Delights, the Crimsettes, and the Queens.

But they had a secret. One the world didn't know. Their union, their marriage, was old news. Still, there was something exhilarating about performing under the big top.

Adrenaline rushed and Jane's hand got clammy. Standing up in front of thousands of people was something Roxie did practically every day. Sure, most of them were numbers on a screen, but that didn't diminish their importance or impact. Jane, on the other hand, was less experienced with being visually consumed.

"You ready?" Toria asked.

Who? Her or Jane?

Everyone had to be on their game.

"Ready," she said and they looked to Jane. "You've been ready for this since you were four years old. Just keep your eyes on Knox."

"I can't—I don't—this is too much. What if it doesn't work out?"

"It did work out, honey." The back of her fingers skimmed down her cheek. "Just like we talked about on Crimson Isle. You thought it wouldn't work out then, now look where we are."

If only they'd known then what they knew now.

"Yeah," Toria said. "You really did find love in paradise. You did it. You found him."

"How you feeling?" she asked. "You ready?" Jane just nodded, still kind of glazed though it appeared more in wonder than in fright. "I'll go first, soften up the crowd. Toria will go next with Ballard and Cam. They're waiting with our dads... unless you need Toria to stay here with you."

"No. No. No," Jane said and swallowed. "That

works."

"Ready?" Toria asked again.

"Ready."

"We'll stand over here," Toria said, leading Jane to the corner that would be behind the double doors when they were open.

On the other side of those doors was her father, waiting to hand her over to the guy she'd already married. Yeah, there was some irony in her father giving permission after the fact. Hell, since when had they been linear? Zairn would play along. Oh, he was good at playing, with her, with the family, with absolutely everyone. Her guy was always top of the league… many, many leagues, actually.

Where was she again? Ah, good. People. Married. She had this. No problem.

There had to be a camera somewhere because she'd been told to face the doors and just nod when ready. And there it was. She moistened her lips and straightened her posture.

Lead with the boobs.

The doors opened, the music started. Her father stepped to the center of the aisle, arm aloft, awaiting hers. This was madness. The people. The music. The flowers… that look on her dad's face. How the hell did this happen? No… uh oh, oh no.

Shit.

She blanched and leaped aside, crowding behind the open door, hiding with her friends.

"What are you—you need to go down there," Toria hissed.

"I can't," she whispered. "I can't, I can't."

"What? Why?" Jane asked, concern as genuine as ever. "You don't want to marry Zairn?"

"Whiplash! We never saw this one coming," Toria said. "Want me to call Dennis? What do we think about Acapulco?"

"Acapulco later…" The music faltered and stopped. Oh, God, her mouth, her chest, this was bad. Breathe. Calm. Breathe. "Shit…"

"Suddenly gone shy? Afraid of the people? Since when have you had stage fright?"

Not a chance of that, she commanded nightclubs full of people at a second's notice these days.

"No, I…" Her heart raced. "Oh…"

"Rox—"

"Lola…" came the shouted drawl from beyond their shield. "Do I have to come get you?"

"Uh, no, dear," she called back. "We're good here. All good. I'll be out in a minute, Casanova."

God, she couldn't even say that without the tightness in her chest growing. It was going to burst. She was going to burst.

"You're going to break his heart?" Jane breathed, her own eyes tearing. "Oh, Roxie…"

"No," she said, circling her lips to pant a little. "No broken hearts." Deep breath. "I'll get it together, just give me a minute."

"That's what the walk is for, to get it together. Just walk, that's all you have to do."

"I… I can't right now." Squeezing her lips together, her cheeks puffed before her admission came out in a long breath. "If I go out there now, like this…" Her volume dropped. "I'll laugh! I can't keep a straight face."

"Oh my God," Jane said.

Toria was less help because she did laugh. "I love it!"

"You can't—I can't… I can't laugh. Stop. Curse you, champagne! Oh, I have to take this seriously. All those people want…"

Reverence. Awe. Dignity. Fuck, why was she

her?

"You can do this…" Though it didn't help much that Toria still struggled with her own amusement. "Take your own advice, just look at Zairn."

She huffed. "Are you crazy? That's not going to help. If I look at him, I'll laugh for sure. He'll be up there, all somber, smooth operator, smoldering and respectable and… I'll be thinking of the last time I had his cock in my mouth." So inappropriate. Seriously. Seriously. She could take this seriously. "Okay…" She rolled her shoulders and tipped her head side to side, limbering up for the prize fight. "I can do this… Easy… Somber." She cleared her throat and blanked her face. "Okay, good, I'm good. Take two."

Jane fluffed at her hair a little. "You've got this."

Roxie stepped out into view of the aisle again. "Okay," she called. This time her father came to her, no chance of backing out again when he snagged her arm. "We're good. Music, maestro."

Cam and Ballard flanked the aisle, waiting to escort Toria. Judging by the looks on their faces, they'd heard some of her exchange with the girls. One smiled and the other scowled, enjoying her in their own ways.

After passing the duo, the room opened up. There were people. Many, many people. As she walked, the true grandeur hit home, it was humbling. That man up there, the one smirking at her—yes, he was smirking—he'd done this for her. This all existed because of them.

Did it matter he hadn't made the calls or attended every planning session? No. The wedding was nothing compared to the life they shared, what they'd been through together, what they'd endured.

He'd done all this for her. Not the wedding, the relationship. He was the reason they made it. Him. Every time he tolerated her flippancy, every time he was patient, he was kind, generous, willing to overlook her failings. He could've walked away any time, could've done better than her for sure. Not "better" per se but definitely easier. On a different path, he could've been with a straightforward woman, someone like Kesley who'd be demure and sophisticated. But no, he put up with her eavesdropping, with her meddling, he enabled her bad habits and her independence. Gave her the latitude to prop up her girls, to fight for them, to win.

The guests smiled and whispered at her, but she didn't acknowledge them, just kept on going, one foot in front of the other. She barely heard the music over the sound of his heart calling to hers.

His smirk faded to something much more profound as he stepped down from the elevated altar to meet them. Her father lifted her veil, it took her a real effort to tear her gaze from Zairn's to accept her dad's kiss. The men shook hands and shared a few words.

When her father went to his seat, Zairn ran the back of his finger down her cheek. "Nice to finally see you." See? Yes, because they'd done feel and hear last night… taste too, mmm. "What was the delay?"

The ball of hilarity she'd squashed down into her gut still hopped and bounced. Man was playing with fire asking for an explanation. If he kept loosening that valve, laughter could explode out of her at any second.

"I was going to laugh. It just hit me, this urge to…" because being with him was filled with surreal moments like this. "I still might so, you know, brace yourself."

His lips curled, lighting his eyes until his own laugh cascaded around her. The most incredible sound…

He cupped her face in both hands to angle her head back. "You want to laugh, Lola Bunny? Laugh," he murmured against her mouth before joining them.

Mm, she could've used a taste of that tongue

before her journey down the—

"Not yet!" Jane's voice echoed from the foyer.

They couldn't see her, maybe Jane had spies. How else would her friend know they were…? Maybe because the room was smiling and clapping. Well, hell, it wouldn't be their wedding without a little drama, would it?

Jane was her own kind of wildcat and took this stuff seriously. Serious enough for all of them. They'd respect that. She really wanted to respect that.

Zairn linked their fingers and led her onto the altar to wait at the side as Toria took her trip down the aisle.

"How's Jane doing?" Zairn murmured, still doing his duty of being focused on Toria though his hand slid down her back to stop just before the ample ruffled skirt.

"Maybe a seven on the Jane scale. Though that's before she's walked out to all these people."

"You're a vision, Roxanna. As stunning today as you were in your Lola pajamas the night we met. I'm one lucky sonofabitch."

She rocked her hip against him. "Smooth talker."

"You sure that thing doesn't have quick access?"

Tipping her head, she met the mischief in his eye. "Get Tripp's permission, did you?"

"No, I thought I'd take a swing at screwing you all by myself."

"I'm a bride," she said as the music changed to Jane's fanfare. Good thing their friend was so eager to marry, she'd talked about her wedding so often that she and Toria knew the details by heart. "You don't screw a bride."

"Bang? Bone? Or am I sticking with the traditional and just fucking you senseless?"

And there was that urge to laugh again.

"You make sweet love to your bride," she teased in a mock player voice. "If she lets you."

"Mm? Bit late to play hard to get when you're wearing the ring, the dress. I'm sure all these people are here for something. Any ideas what they're waiting for?"

"Yes," she said, her shoulders rising with her inhale. Breath held, she anticipated… "For her."

TWENTY

TALK ABOUT A VISION and what a gown. Jane's voluminous full skirt beneath the diamond-encrusted bodice—yes, they were real diamonds—completed the fairytale look.

Roxie went one step closer to the perfection and delight of her friend emerging from the foyer at the head of the aisle.

This was it: Jane's wedding day. Of every memory in life, now and in the future, this would be a pinnacle snapshot. Beautiful, precious, incredible Jane. Fulfilling her dream was a humbling moment.

Hand tucked in the crook of her father's elbow, Jane glided down the aisle, smooth, effortless, buoyant, luminescent.

One. Two. Pink spots fell from above. Another. Another. Dozens. Hundreds. What the hell was… The whole room was being showered in… cherry blossoms. My God, the man was good. That wasn't her or Jane, it had to be Knox. Astounding. Outstanding.

Her friend's delight came in a gasp and slight

falter. Basking in the romance raining down upon them, her joyful laugh floated through the room.

They'd come a long way from their early days in Chicago eating cereal for dinner and drinking cheap wine from a box. She pulled her and Zairn's joined hands to her belly, gaze never leaving Jane.

Knox was there, descending to receive the hand of his bride with such pride, love bloomed in her heart. It was something. Getting this view, from this angle, being up close, was poignant, like living in a movie. A tear tumbled from her lashes as Toria blocked her view.

Right. Wedding.

Why was her friend so—

"Flowers," Toria whispered.

Flow—the bouquet, yes. Toria took both her and Jane's flowers and went to stand on the other side of Jane. Zairn's finagling reminded her to turn her back on the room. They'd gone through all of this. Rehearsed it. Her, Jane, and the other women yesterday before her bachelorette party. Funny that her groom wasn't the one knocking her on her ass, Jane had delivered the real killer blow. What a picture.

Happy to take the lead, her guy was there, still holding her hand, poised to direct. Wherever the maneuver, she'd go, so long as it was with him. That shifted her wonder. Casanova, there, at her side, intent on the officiant's opening speech. From the backstreets of Chicago to Pleasantropolis, New York City. Okay, maybe not Pleasantropolis for everyone, but no one could deny her life these days was pleasant.

"...if anyone objects to either of these unions, speak now or forever hold your peace," the officiant said.

Damnit, why hadn't she been thinking? What a perfect moment for drama! They should've set something up to make sure—

"I object!"

Ooo, that got the place roaring instantly. Whispers joined their turn to the congregation and, who was on her feet? Yeah, that was Roux. Rourke slouched at his wife's side, finger curled over his mouth, yeah, good try, that didn't hide his laugh. What were the chances he'd prodded his wife into it? Pretty good.

"You object?" the officiant asked, flummoxed.

Fair response. These objections couldn't come every day. Presumably. How would she know? Crimson should get into the wedding game.

"I love them both," Roux declared.

"Both…" The officiant stuttered. "You're in love with both grooms?"

"Not the men." Roux rolled her eyes. "Both women. I love them both. Those guys up there better treat them right, or they'll be answering to me."

As Roux sat, she winked. Yep, her friend had read her mind. Jane was probably having a coronary. Zairn wouldn't care, drama happened and he dealt with it. Knox may be building up a steam, but Jane would work that out of him later.

"Should…" the officiant started, "should I keep going?"

"Yes," she said, wrapping both arms around Zairn's, anchoring herself as she twisted to the room again. "Any more objections? Do we need a talking stick? Form an orderly line if my hubby's exes need to plead their cases. I could very easily have drugged and taken advantage of him, might be you're in with a shot."

A few whispers and head shakes rippled through the room, but no one else spoke out.

"She's kidding," Zairn said, yanking her hard against him. "Behave yourself, Lola."

Yeah, yeah, he loved her, even when she was naughty. Sometimes because of it.

"That's not what your smile says, Casanova."

It was coming closer, his mouth on a trajectory for hers when…

Jane yelped. "Not yet."

"Right, not yet," she said and bumped Zairn again. "Sex pest. You heard the woman, keep those babies to yourself until later." Her focus landed on their emcee—was he an emcee? "Please carry on. We don't have all day."

"Sex and drama," Zairn muttered.

She peeked up. "Less of one and more of the other?"

"Mm hmm."

Drama didn't bother him. By now, he was used to Roux and the other rabble rousers in her pack. Others may not be accustomed to such spectacle, but to have those whispers and curiosities following them for the rest of the day, yeah, that was Crimson gold. She just couldn't help herself. The thrill of Zairn's utter acceptance, not only acceptance, but love, boosted her excitement. This guy was her husband. It didn't matter what happened that day, or any other, they'd always have love.

After Jane and Knox exchanged vows, all eyes fell on them. Yep, this was it. Not particularly nervous, she wasn't sure just how deep they might get while under such examination. They shared honesty as a couple. They didn't always share it with the world at large.

As they faced each other, her world narrowed to one. Him. Only him. They were in fancy clothes, surrounded by luxury, scrutinized to the hilt, but they may as well have been naked in their sex sheets.

"We never put boundaries on each other," she said. It might be traditional for the groom to go first, but this was her Casanova. She would never top whatever came from his mouth. "Constraints, limitations, they don't exist between us. No matter what happens, we stand proud beside each other even when there are oceans between us.

"You're a man few people know, and even fewer know well. I don't understand what I did to deserve this, you, your love, and maybe I never will. You have this way..." Sinking deeper into him, inching closer, she rested both hands on his chest. On instinct, his arms coiled around her. "You look at me and I understand. You hold me and I'm saved. You only have to say my name and I know what's in your head.

"This is innate, that's what you said once, that this is instinctual. And that's the truth. I live it every minute. Being yours. My love for you is forever and even that doesn't feel like enough. I couldn't exist without you. You are the sun, my oxygen, the life blood that rushes through me. You're the future, and all I need in the now. Every part of me was created to be with you and I always will be. Every second until eternity, I will be yours."

The collective sigh of the room was encouraging, though it didn't seem that Zairn heard it.

"Roxanna..." On an exhale, he grew discerning. "What can I possibly say that would be an honest measure of how much I love you?" His lips met and he breathed for a couple of beats. "Words. Actions. Nothing I can give you will match how you overwhelm me every day. If this is luck, it better never run out. I wouldn't just cease to exist without you, I'd take the whole damn world with me, and you know it.

"Your smile. Your grace. Your gentle touch... I could never have known a woman like you existed; there is no other woman like you. From the second we met, you enlivened me. You stir my blood as much today as you did then. That will never change. You're pure truth. True passion. My delight." They shared a smile. With each passing second, more and more of her weight relied on him to keep her upright. Damn the dress. "You crawled inside me, Lola. Took over my body, my heart.

I will never be the same. You sharpened my wit, my vision. You make me a better man.

"The world makes new sense to me. You are now, and always will be, my single guiding force. The rest of it can go to hell, I don't give a damn. Everything that came before was a prelude to you. Loving you is what I was made for; being with you is my life purpose. You…" He cupped her face, "are the sun which my world revolves around."

"And you are mine," she whispered.

His lips touched hers, just the slightest brush and then they ebbed. They'd probably never shared a kiss so delicate, nor one so powerful.

The whole room swooned.

"We have an audience," she said to the officiant though it would be picked up by the microphones projecting their voices. Yes, there were microphones secreted in the flowers. That's how many people had shown up to witness this. "It's when he does his best work."

"I do my best work for you, baby."

Pushing up to her tiptoes, it was almost impossible to resist his mouth. She only managed it because although he bowed, he kept it just out of reach.

"You're too hot and rich for your own good," she whispered. "You know that?"

"Mm hmm."

Curse her lack of foresight. Quick access in her wedding dress should've been a primary demand. If she had to go upstairs and take it off, even without being explicit about her purpose, Zairn would follow. This was a SIAG day, that's "sex is almost guaranteed" day. He'd know if she was alone, in private… and naked. Though, in fairness, with Zairn, whenever he decided it was one of those days, it instantly became one. Man knew how to talk, and tantalize, his way into a woman's panties and now all that superpower was reserved for her.

Rings.

"With this ring, I thee wed…"

The best men produced the rings and words were said. Wedding bands were the one thing taken care of by the grooms. Well, groom, with Jane not knowing her guy would be a groom that day and all.

The black band with its ring of rubies gave her further proof this was the right guy. That certainty didn't come in its shine or likely high cost, no, that came in how well it suited her. Beautiful. Unique. Different. Them.

His was just the same only thicker, the stones square and flat. They matched in case anyone was keeping score. Before the Empress Ruby, she hadn't been one for wearing rings. Now she felt naked without it. Already the band felt at home. By wearing it, she was more complete.

The bow on top came with the hands that curved around her waist and squeezed. Zairn teased her like that in bed too, when she was on top and he wanted to possess her.

She loved it when he possessed her.

"And now…" the officiant said, "you may kiss your brides."

Three pairs of eyes went to Jane.

On a giggle, she nodded once. "Now's the time."

TWENTY-ONE

THE ROOM ERUPTED in a blast of cheers and hilarity as each man complied. A kiss. So simple; something she took for granted. Zairn was already her husband, he'd kissed her as her spouse many, many times—done a helluvalot more than kiss her.

Technically, they'd had their wedding night, been on honeymoon… Right then, that didn't matter. The moment was profound. This wasn't only for them, it was for everyone. The world knew. No more secrets. No more hiding.

Clarity awakened her to Zairn's urgency that they be joined, whether the masses knew it or not. The link of marriage was different. It wasn't easy to explain the wholesomeness of it, the unity, the depth of commitment it required. Now she understood why it was so important to Jane too.

So much time and energy had been focused on making the event happen. Not just the details, but the talk of it, the conversation, the questions. For so long it had been wedding, wedding, wedding. She'd lost count of how many times it came up online and in real life. The media, her streaming viewers, everyone wanted to talk about it. With all the talk, it had become almost unreal.

Now, as the music rose, that was it. Deed done. This life event would never happen again.

Yeah, they still had a reception ahead, a meal, a party, but… What would they do with their time now? What would they talk about? Was that just it?

Zairn released her as someone touched her back. Jane. She immediately turned into her friend's embrace. Being up there together, doing this together… They'd have to renew their vows when Toria got hitched, just to be up there as a trio.

The men shook hands, there was back slapping and laughter as she got kisses and hugs from everyone up there, even Ballard, maybe he was drunk already. You'd think Knox might be the hold out, but he was a goddamn Collier, they learned presentation and appearances before they left the womb.

"The register is just here," the officiant said.

Off Knox and Cam went with Jane ensconced between them. She wasn't so quick off the mark.

"Uh, how does this work?" she whispered to the men on either side of her, watching her friend's progress. "We've already signed one of these."

"And we're smart enough to have a dummy one," Ballard said. "Make like it's real."

Huh, the Colliers weren't the only ones privy to the necessity of presentation and appearances.

Jane laughed with the officiant, still with that aura of pure joy. Her hand rose until her knuckles landed on Zairn's abs.

"Let's give them a minute."

Every detail was important to her friend. Jane would remember every second of this day forever. Letting her have those moments with her groom meant so much.

"They can take their time," Zairn said, scooping a hand around her opposite cheek to steal her focus.

Mmm, and her mouth.

Kissing they were good at. Making out too. Really any activity that involved any kind of bodily contact.

What was getting to him right then? The dress? The hair? Had she ever understood what about her turned him on? Not particularly. Perhaps the pheromones. He sure drugged her with a dose of his every once in a while. Did hers react to his and cause… this?

At Crimson, in the nights, sometimes they'd talk, sometimes they'd flirt, other times they'd use their mouths for a much better purpose.

Most of the time, she was the initiator. Zairn never shied with his hands, they often ended up under her skirt or anywhere else they pleased.

And she loved it.

How he touched her and owned her and demanded her compliance while surrendering his in return. The gentle ebb of his kiss returned in a slow, teasing retreat that sparked her desperation to take things up a gear.

When he finally took them for good, his fingertips trailed down her bare arms.

"Want to do this here or move it upstairs?"

Grr, her guy was ready to—why were her fingers on the buttons of his shirt? His jacket and vest were undone, open, granting access to her wandering hands. Had she…? Wow, brazen. Go her.

Instincts were right on the ball. A whisper of a chance at skin-on-skin contact and primal reflex did its thing. Stripping him naked was apparently so second nature that it happened subconsciously.

"I've missed touching you."

Though she maybe should've considered that her parents were watching from a few feet away. What the hell, they were probably chatting it up. They wouldn't care. Where did they think their grandchildren would come from?

"Upstairs it is," her guy said, grabbing her fingers between his.

"Not a chance, you two," Ballard said, blocking their way. "You've got a captive audience ready for more."

"We're ready for more too," Zairn said and tried to sidestep him. "And we're happy to be captive."

For each other. His eagerness was flattering, though Ballard had a point.

"Gonna do this to Jane?" Ballard asked, eyes on hers.

Ouch, low blow, but the man made his point.

She exhaled. "He's right."

"We haven't seen each other for two weeks," Zairn said to his best man.

Guy wasn't buying it. "'Cept last night."

"We didn't see each other last night."

That was no lie.

"Got yours though, didn't you?" The bodyguard crooked a brow. "Think I'm that dumb? You two in the same building…" He did know them rather well, maybe too well. "With that out the way, what do you plan to do upstairs?"

"We'll tell you how it goes when we come back down."

"You leave this room now, we won't see you again this week."

"That's a lot of cuddling," Roxie said.

"And the rest," Ballard replied. "All this pomp and money spent? You gonna walk out on it."

They couldn't exactly say a person only had one wedding when this was her and Zairn's second.

"Suppose he's right… I can't leave until someone comments on my shoes."

Ballard's scowl was reassuring. "What's wrong with your shoes, Little Rox?"

"Jane has diamonds on her dress," Roxie said, gathering up her skirt just enough to poke her foot out the bottom. "She's not the only one with bling."

Zairn laughed.

Ballard shook his head. "Are those…"

"Ruby slippers, just like the Wicked Witch." She rolled her ankle left and right, round and round. "Good for the brand, Casanova?"

"You're a good girl."

"Enough to earn another kiss?"

Dipping down, coming closer, the twist of the smile on her beautiful man's face promised way more than a fleeting kiss. For now, for forever, for—

"Rox!" Jane called, still beaming. Ah, Ballard saved by the bride. One of them. "You have to come over here." She gestured. "Come over here."

Tightening her hold on Zairn's hand, she forced him to follow her over to the paperwork. "Duty calls."

"You have to witness this," Jane said. "You and Zairn. We'll do yours."

"Symmetry," Roxie said, refastening her guy's buttons. Putting him back together without taking advantage was a real downer on the day. "Classy."

This wouldn't be the moment she revealed to Jane that her and Zairn's certificate was a fake. Actually, this was the moment that guaranteed she'd never reveal to anyone that her and Zairn's certificate was a fake.

She signed, he signed, everyone signed.

"Can you believe this?" Jane said when the four guys gathered for another back-smacking laugh session.

"We're married! It's here, it's—" Her inhale was a pant of disbelief. "Thank you. Thank you! I can't—this is incredible, amazing, we're… I can't believe we're married! I'm a wife! We're wives!"

"Yes," she said, doing her best to get close enough for the semblance of a hug.

Wasn't so easy with Jane's incredible skirt. She had layers, but Jane's dress was something else. More like art than attire.

The noise rose with every second. No matter the size of the space, thirteen hundred people made themselves known. In there, much like at the club of an evening, a whisper didn't exist.

"We'll do the walk back down the aisle and the drinks reception will start while we're getting pictures," Jane said. "You're getting pictures. Oh, uh, I don't know if the photographers—"

"Bought and paid for, honey. You think we'd forget to guarantee your memories? What will you show your grandchildren if you don't have pictures? Knox will be senile and useless by then, it will be all on you to animate the dream."

Jane sort of quivered as her color rose. "Grandchildren?"

"Sure! You're one step closer," Roxie said. "You've got the guy. You live together. We've taken care of marriage…" She leaned in to whisper, "Next is babies."

"Babies."

Her friend's conflict was clear. Jane would want to squee over the possibility but had only that morning thought her guy wanted to break up. Sure, he'd proved that wasn't true… Would he be ready for the offspring conversation? One step at a time.

"Aisle walk, cheering, pictures, we can do this. Let's get our guys."

Jane caught her hand before she took a step. "Rox, after the pictures, we have to do a thing."

"A thing?" Not one to hesitate, she'd be up for whatever. Her threshold for the shocking was way higher than Jane's. "Okay. With the guys?"

"Just us. We talked about the—"

"Ah, our first costume change?"

"Costume and… a little extra." Jane squealed and raised her shoulders before passing her by. "Knox, honey…"

In response to his bride, her friend's new husband left his buddies just like that. Good, Knox was doing okay.

"Blossom…?"

"Can they leave it?" Jane asked.

"Leave what? You can have anything you want."

"The blossom. I want it to stay on the floor."

God, it would be everywhere, and probably a slip hazard. That didn't matter more than the romance. Dutiful Knox was good to cover litigation costs.

Speaking of dutiful… Where was her husband?

There he was, with Ballard a few feet away, smiling at her. Creep. She didn't have to call or go to him. Nope. She spun on the spot to sashay slowly toward the aisle. He'd catch up. Man never could resist her caboose.

TWENTY-TWO

DRINKS AND DINNER came after the big reveal. An apparel change alone wasn't good enough for Jane. No, they were out there more than a little while with makeup artists, stylists, colorists, the whole roster. On their return, she was a brunette again, just like the old days. When she and Zairn got together. And the look on his face when she returned to him… Yeah, no medals for noticing his obvious gratitude. Nostalgia? Maybe. But pleasing him was some kick.

During the wedding planning stages, she'd suggested, requested, her gown be red. Yeah, Jane didn't go for that. This was the compromise. In the change for dinner, she got to wear the red dress, a miniaturized version of her wedding gown, that went perfect with her slippers. Score one for diplomacy.

Jane maintained the theme. Her miniaturized dress was iceberg blue. Embroidered with fewer diamonds, though no less striking, the color created an optical illusion. Blue? White? Who knew?

Feeding so many people was a colossal task and

the Grand staff were impeccable in every way. Because Bastian, the hotel's owner, was in the room? Maybe. Either way, she'd make sure they were tipped ridiculously well.

Who was she kidding? Zairn would've taken care of that already. He'd have done it before the big day and would no doubt do the same again after. Knowing their group, as she did, Knox had probably tipped too… and his dad… maybe his brother.

Hell, this was a lucrative event for staff. Wonder if there were any openings.

Cam gave a speech. Ballard gave a speech. Everyone laughed. Joy filled the room.

More than for just herself, she almost wished the day would never end. Each time she glimpsed Jane, the reward was right there.

People came to the top table, frequently. During the meal, guests were told several times to take their seats. The mood had a lot to answer for; everyone's smiles rode high.

Dessert had been cleared and another round of drinks served. She didn't partake. The glass was there, but with the speeches over, they'd be dancing soon. Getting up in front of the room with a full gut would be a mistake.

At that particular moment, Zairn was talking to a trio of guys who'd appeared on their platform a while ago. Too long ago. Her guy's forearm rested across her lap, though he was twisted the other way. Like being in the club, only this time there was light and conversation and far less leg in the room.

Be polite. Be patient.

Though were these guys being polite or patient? If she heard the word "projections" one more time… This was not a business day. It was their wedding day, as much Zairn's as hers. Her husband. Her public husband.

Her no-longer-a-secret husband.

They didn't have two chairs. Another Jane addition that won her extra points. On the couch in the club, they sat thigh to thigh, and there, at their wedding feast, they did the same. No light, no air, passed between them.

One feature of her layered skirt hadn't been exploited. This one did have quick emergency access. The layers weren't fully stitched as they had been in the wedding gown. She'd been waiting for the most opportune moment to educate her husband. There it was, upon them. Easing one layer this way and another that, the table concealed her actions. Some things were kept only for her spouse.

He was still talking when she picked up his hand to guide his palm to her flesh. Nice and high on her thigh, skimming it up and down on the—

Zairn's attention flew around to her. One glance down and then to her face, ah, check that surprise!

"That's a suspender belt." Shock. Horror. "You're wearing a suspender belt?"

"I am," she said, relishing his astonishment.

"You're wearing lingerie?"

"For one night only. All you had to do was wait eighteen months, buy me lots of jewelry, fuck me a few hundred times, oh, and marry me, to see it."

"Shit, are you a doppelganger? Did I marry the right Lola?"

Once again, her life choices paid off. See how much more effective it was because she didn't do it every day?

"Special treat, just for you. From Lola Bunny upstairs to leather and lace in the ballroom. Not bad, huh?"

"There's leather involved?" he asked, arching a brow as he leaned in.

"You'll have to wait and find out, won't you?"

Instead of a kiss, he left her hanging and stood, sweeping up a flute of champagne and a spoon. The ting of the two coming together, surprisingly, did its thing to silence the room, eventually.

A tech guy hurried over in a crouch to give Zairn a microphone. Yep, their wedding was so crazy that it required tech people.

"Thank you," Zairn said, putting his champagne on the table by hers. "I told Lola once that the groom doesn't give a speech at the wedding reception. And she loves proving me wrong so… my gift to you, baby…" Laughter rippled through the room. Damn, did he have to be so fine and funny too? Someone should marry that guy. "I'll be brief, talking for too long about my relationship tends to get me into trouble."

Oh, so long ago, man, was she glad for every second with him.

He continued. "You may be surprised to learn that the world-at-large doesn't know the full truth of our relationship. Shocking, right? Sometimes feels like you can't turn around without seeing one or both of us…"

"They see more of me, Casanova, they prefer my cleavage to yours."

Zairn took the microphone closer to his lips. "So do I." Haha, oh, so proud of him. "I couldn't let today go by without thanking the most important person in my life." It didn't matter who else was there. When he looked down at her, he beheld only her. "This day last year…" And she'd hoped they might get through the party without recalling this day last year. "I broke your heart."

"I broke yours first."

She had no microphone, but he would hear her.

"Walking away from you was the most difficult thing I've ever done." On an exhale, he addressed the room again. "Roxanna and I fit together from the minute we met. Touching her, being with her, as far as the world was concerned, crossed some line. With women, before Roxanna, in business, in family, there were uncrossable lines."

"Boundaries," she said almost behind her glass.

His head didn't move, but his lips betrayed he'd heard her.

He kept on going. "It's never been like that with her. It's cliché to say I knew from the minute we met, and that wouldn't be completely true given the first thing we did was argue."

"Shocker!" came a call from the crowd.

Rourke, that was Rourkey-Baby, and he was sitting there all smug, enjoying his laugh.

"We're solid and that's no exaggeration. You've seen the news reports, things written about us… Things we may have accidently streamed…"

"My fault," she called to the room and held up her glass in admission.

Though it came up so regularly that the masses already knew.

"I'm not sorry," he said, once again looking at her. "Not for a second of it." Because each of their seconds together brought them to that moment, to their love, their happiness, their forever. "For that brief spell, when I walked away, I could never free myself. Even if you hadn't come back to me, I'd still have loved you, then, now, forever. What we have, Lola, is bigger than just you and me. Being with you… I thank whatever fate set me on this path. Without you, life would have no meaning. With you, I know there's nothing I can't face, that we can't face or overcome. As long as we have each other, everything else is meaningless. Nothing has power over this except you. Your heart, your love, it fuels me every day. I want to make you proud, baby, to make you happy.

"This is just our first step. Today we're renewed and can finally tell everyone the truth." Uh, no. About their marriage? No! "We can confess to our friends and families that… you made the first move on me." Phew! The room's laughter echoed again, it kept going until her cheeks ached with the grin that plumped them. "Okay, okay, but seriously…" he quieted the room. "You saved my life with that kiss, Roxanna Kyst. Who I was, the way I was going then, everything was about to fall apart. I was shattered, broken, and you sailed on in with that incredible smile and the caboose I can't resist…" See, she knew him. "You're pure energy, pure light, and every single thing I've built has been for you. Doesn't matter that I didn't know you then, I know you now, and I know it's for you. All of it, Roxanna. I get out of bed every day for you. Eat, drink, sleep you. There's no tomorrow, no yesterday, only what we have right here and now. And as long as you're happy, nothing else matters to me."

Rising, she cast her glass aside and moved the microphone to free his mouth for hers. Their guests had gotten more than one show that day. Hell, did she care? This was her guy and she'd take every available chance to appreciate him.

His tongue touched hers one last time before retreating.

"You really do do your best work with an audience, Casanova."

He laughed. "I do my best work for you."

"You got the girl," she murmured. "No one is ever taking me away."

In the next kiss, his arm locked around her, lifting her from her feet to take their kiss to his height. The guests may be applauding, cheering, but they couldn't keep going all night. What a damn shame. Hmm, wonder how long it would take to clear the whole place.

Someone prodded her, jarring her from the kiss. Toria.

"Uh, they're playing your song."

Song? What did?

Oh, the dance floor was dark, the band illuminated.

"Ah!" In her joy, she kissed Zairn again, quick this time. "Now you have to dance with me."

"We're not at work."

"For maybe the first time. You're just as obligated here," she said, linking their fingers when he put her back on her feet. "Now everyone gets to see."

The meal sundries had been whooshed away by their army of servers. The cherry blossoms would be taken home by all on shoes and shawls, but the dance floor was clear of it at least.

Zairn overtook her to lead the way onto the empty floor. They stopped in the middle and boom, spotlight. Right there in the glow from above, he turned, yanked, and then she was against him, in his arms. Ah, the flip move from bed diversified to vertical. Impressive.

"Ladies and gentlemen, Mr. and Mrs. Zairn Lomond."

Okay, she'd let that one slide, because he was too good at this. Her forearms against him, she pushed herself close as he squeezed. Everyone would recognize the music from their Rome dance, that had since aired to the world, but it still meant more to them than anyone could ever know. That night was the first they…

"We should do this every year."

"We do it every week," Zairn said. "Any time you want to dance—"

"The wedding," she said. "Jane's too beautiful to only be a bride once."

Something crossed his expression as his eyes

moved away for a moment before returning. "You have an impervious quality that makes me forget to compliment you like I should."

"You are leaning hard on the nostalgia."

"I love Jane. She's a sweet girl, deserving, loyal, beautiful."

"Buyer's remorse?"

He snickered. "That's just it, baby. You're you and deserve nothing less than she does. The way you look at her, the love you have for her, she wants you to be as happy. We both do."

"We're family," she said. "All of us. We're happy together."

"Knox loves her no more than I love you. I'd argue he loves Jane less, but I am better at everything and like to win."

"You never win with me."

"I don't. Know why that is?"

"Yeah." She rubbed her cheek against him. "Because I have the reins."

"At home and in the office. Here, there, and everywhere."

"What is it you and your boys say? All is fair in love and business," she said and slid her hands higher. "Knox likes straightforward, likes satisfying Jane's needs, even the crazy ones, and he never apologizes for it."

"You think I apologize for loving you?"

"No! I'm just a little more complicated."

"A little?"

Okay, buddy, laugh it up. "You wouldn't want this if you didn't want complicated," she said. "You're not so straightforward yourself."

"We're talking about you here."

"Oh, are we? My mistake."

"You want to get married again, Lola B? We'll get married again. Hell, we'll do it every other day if it makes you happy. Jane deserves that. You deserve that too."

"Nothing wrong with my self-esteem."

"You don't like praise either."

The sterner note of his gaze hailed back to the very moment she'd said something similar to him.

"Oh my God, you're clapping back to something I said—when did I say that?"

"Vegas."

"That's right," the agreement left on her breath. "Come to the fiftieth."

"Mm hmm."

"And you, oh, oh, you said you had a condition." Her nose wrinkled. "Were you telling me to get tested?"

"We hadn't had sex then."

"No, we had not…" Although… "Not in real life, maybe in my head a few times."

His laugh was always a reward. "Liar. I was fantasizing about fucking you long before you thought it about me."

"Hey, I was never against sleeping with you, I was just less… eager than some of your fans." Like her BFFs. Hamming it up, she batted her eyelashes at him. "Don't I make up for that now?"

"Hmm…"

"Now I think about having sex with you all the time. I'm thinking about it right now."

"That dress does have quick access. Shouldn't have shown me that if you didn't want it exploited."

"Exploit it any time, Scroogey. I'm your number one fan."

"Don't forget I'm yours after Roxiverse airs and your popularity soars. Number one topic, rain or shine, everywhere I go it's 'Roxie this…' 'Roxie that…' You'll get bigger when you rule mainstream media."

"Ah, so that's why you married me."

"For the street cred? You figured me out, baby."

"If I was straightforward like Jane, you wouldn't have your in with all my girls and their gossip. I know how you love to chat about their issues and get involved fixing their lives and their loves. Talking into the wee hours, sharing their hair and makeup tips has to be one of the highlights you get with me. We should do that more often."

"Grand romantic gestures would be so much easier."

"Nah, they're exhausting." On a bluster of breath, her forehead dropped against him for a beat. "You trying to decipher crazy hints, me upset when you don't hear them. You plan some big thing and I have to react, oooh, ahh…" she mocked herself. "Then there's the people and the press… Can't we just have sex in public or something if you need a big gesture? Wouldn't that be simpler?"

"Been talking to Roux?"

"Shame she and I are different too. I prefer having you to myself."

All to herself. Him. Them. Love, marriage, and happily ever after, saved for him alone.

He kissed her head. "Have you had a good day?"

"It's not over yet, Scroogey." She beamed. "I have plans for later."

"You want to get married again?"

"Heard third time's a charm. Not tonight though, we need to set another date if we want more presents."

They'd asked people to donate to specific charities in lieu of actual presents. No charity would refuse that gift twice.

"Lola—"

"My friends are important to me. They're important to you. That's what wins you points, Casanova. You care about what I care about. You listen. You allow me so much freedom." That wasn't about geography or money, his support allowed her to reach every peak. "Knox does what makes Jane happy and that involves public displays. Want to know where our power is? How you can match him?"

"Tell me."

Rising on her tiptoes, she stayed close, begging him to keep their balance. "Right here," she whispered. "When I have you all to myself."

The public bayed for Zairn. Always had. He gave the masses just enough to whet their appetites while maintaining the enigma.

He kissed her forehead. "Any time you want me, baby."

"You give me so much more than I give you."

"Sometimes you forget how much time I've spent overseas." She didn't get it. "I've been everywhere, Lo. Everywhere. I guarantee there's only one you, I know it. What you give me is irreplaceable. You're the world, baby. The whole world."

"It feels unreal sometimes, doesn't it? What if I wake up tomorrow and you're gone?"

"Then charge your phone, 'cause I promise you I'm trying to call."

Moving to the music, she rested her head against him. There were others around, on the dance floor. The music wound between them, keeping them all together, even while apart. Their friends, their families and colleagues, everyone was there to celebrate love with her and Jane and their beaus. And where there was one good friend…

"Just so you know, we'll definitely be getting married again at least once. We'll have to when Toria finds her Prince Charming," she said. "That's a necessity. Keeps everything fair."

"Toria's wedding? I dread to think. What will that involve? I'm guessing it's not the fairytale dress and a shower of petals."

"Don't be a party pooper, you never know. Could be a naked wedding."

"Then we're talking a vastly reduced guest list. Don't much want to see all my guys' girls naked." He scowled. "Don't want to see your sister and mom naked either."

"Mom's got a great body, she's really active."

"Are you trying to convince me I need to see your mother naked?"

"Convince? No. But would give you a preview of what you have to look forward to."

"Seeing your mom naked?"

His tease earned a nudge though they stayed connected. "You better still be screwing me when I'm her age."

"Okay, well, she can come, if you're adamant."

"Know who's not invited?"

"Dunlap?" he asked. Was he even in the room? There hadn't been time to take a lap. Would probably take a couple of hours, or a whole day, to give everyone a few seconds. "Salad?"

"Ogilvie."

That flattened his affect. "Agreed."

"Of course…" Straightening her arms, she rested her elbows against his shoulders. "We could have a rehearsal naked wedding. All alone."

"We might need more than one."

"Mm, maybe."

"For extra practice…" he said, "we shouldn't stay out too late tonight."

Yeah, when she got caught up in the club, when the mood was high, she could dance until the sun came up.

That night was meant for something else.

"Jane and Knox will cut their cake, we'll bus

everyone to the club… We have one more costume change. For public consumption. You get a special reveal later."

"That a promise?"

"Unless I get a better offer." Her eyes wandered like maybe she was checking out the competition. This was Zairn-damn-Lomond, there was no such thing. "Odds are in your favor so far."

And they'd continue to be. Happily ever after didn't mean happy every minute, she was smart enough to know that. Right then though, being with him, surrounded by friends, she couldn't imagine life getting much better.

TWENTY-THREE

THE FIRST BUS, or maybe two, had already gone. There was no particular need for them to rush, or for Jane to be in a flap. You know, it looked, from an outsider's point of view, that she was in a flap. With Jane the term was "organized chaos." Her anxiety played out on her face, in her fidgeting, a need to move and be moving. But inside, Jane knew exactly what she was doing and definitely had a plan.

Bringing their weddings together might've saved the woman from a breakdown. Doing this once rather than twice relieved some of the pressure. While her friend's brain knew the script, her body burned calories cranking up the adrenaline.

Guests went left and right, closing off her view of Jane, but opening one of her other girls: Roux, Lilya, and Sway. Intriguing. Close quarters. Scrutiny going this way and that… Damn, the cat needed to be satisfied. Never one to miss an escapade, she went to join them.

"You three look like you're brewing a caper."

"Might be."

"I want in," she said. "What's the plan?"

"We're observing the talent. Trying to figure out if those two are together…"

From the nod at a couple standing close, touching, smiling, not quite comfortable, but close to it, she did her own pondering.

"Are they?" Lilya asked.

"I have no idea who those two people are," she admitted.

That was sort of a common theme. Everyone was nice, polite, congratulatory. More faces were familiar than not. Though that didn't mean she really knew them. A lot of Rouge and CollCom folk she may have seen in passing. No way had she conversed with all these people previously.

Telling the coordinator that her list consisted of seven people wasn't a joke. Outside their guy/girl posse, that honestly had been it. She did work for, or with, Rouge and their various offshoots now. Zairn's colleagues were hers too. At some point, she'd corner him to ask how many names he knew. Ugh, what was the point? This was Zairn, he'd know everyone's names.

"And we're trying to figure out which of our single girls we can hook up with the super hottie over there," Roux said, twisting a little to bob her chin toward the corner.

Discreet was so unlike her. Hilarious that—wait. The super hottie…

Ah, interesting.

Leaving the ladies without a word, her eyes stayed set on the man propping up one of the perimeter columns.

He spotted her but didn't react, which was probably why her smile did such a bad job of hiding itself.

"Well, I'll be damned," Roxie said, stopping just

in front of him. He hadn't flinched. "You are alive! Alive and here. Didn't expect that." And from him, the unexpected was kind of a given. "Are you going to kiss me or say congratulations?"

"Hair thing makes you look like a diva."

"Brooding in the corner makes you look like a terrorist," she said and swept her hair from her shoulder. "And I am a diva now."

"You always were." Good thing she knew him well enough to recognize the joke through that deadpan expression. "Congratulations."

"That wasn't so hard, was it?" She steadied herself with a hand on his arm while pushing to her tiptoes to accept his kiss on her cheek. "Want to dance?"

Leveling his gaze over her head, he just kept on examining the crowd. "Don't push it."

"Okay, then come meet him."

"I don't want to meet him. Did I see that dickhead Porter around?"

"He's not a dickhead and you may have done. He's here. Along with a lot of other people. It's not easy to keep track of thirteen hundred-odd guests. You didn't sit with family."

"I didn't want to sit with family."

Lips sealed, she inhaled through her nose and let the breath out slowly. "Always Sad Sack Sam."

"I'm perfectly fine—why are you doing this in LA?"

Not so flat now, his confusion was almost affront as his focus went up and around the room again.

"Where should we have done it? Chicago?" she asked. "Not like I'll believe you were sitting around there waiting for my wedding day. Wherever we did it, you would've had to travel. What am I talking about? You love traveling, especially if it's in a direction opposite to your family."

"I don't like LA."

"You don't like anywhere." Okay, that maybe wasn't true. "I'm surprised you've ever been here. Have you ever been here?" Truthfully, he had probably been everywhere. "Why would you have cause to hang out in LA?"

"You quit your job."

Was he just ignoring her completely? No change there then.

"I got a new job," she declared, maintaining her smile.

"You moved a thousand miles."

"Depends how you travel."

"You left your girls."

"They moved with me."

"You left Porter."

"Who you don't even like and that was way before I met Zairn." At least a couple of months. "He had nothing to do with it. It's a little late to be voicing objections, don't you think? Maybe if you called more, we could've had this conversation, oh, I don't know, a year ago."

And it was then, on softening just a fraction, that his scowl faded to concern and his eyes dropped to hers.

"You changed yourself, Talks-Alot. You remember your promise to me when I left?"

"Yes, I remember. And I didn't change, I grew. If I am a different person now, I'm a better one, a happier one." She snagged his hand and went in close. "I've never been happier, Sam. I love him. I love our life. He's good for me and I'm good for him."

"Hasn't stopped him screwing around."

"That was bullshit. He's never cheated on me. The media stuff is, it's pantomime. Come on, saying something out loud doesn't make it true. You know I'd never stand for that shit with a guy if it was real. Trust me, it isn't. He's never even met that woman."

"Then he has enemies."

"Which come with the territory. Success often breeds contempt." On a blink, her lips met with a startling truth. "Man, I sound all grown up."

He breathed out a laugh and caught the back of her head to pull her against him. He held her there a second, pressing his mouth to the top of her head.

"You weren't supposed to do that either, Talks-Alot."

"Stop calling me that."

"Why? It's true."

"How would you know? You've been off radar for two years."

Relaxing, he guided her head from his chest to read her gaze. "If that name didn't still fit, hellfire would be raining down. And trust me, I've seen that shit, the LA pace isn't it."

She laughed. "You'd probably prefer hellfire."

"Damn right I would."

Time to try again. "Come meet him."

"If he wants to meet me, he knows where I am."

"He doesn't actually." She gestured behind and around without turning. "Did I mention there are several hundred people here?"

"Hangers-on."

"Some, but most of them genuinely care about Zairn. Security was tight. You don't have to worry about—"

"BKS," he said, his gaze narrowing. "And Ryder Stone is here."

"Yes."

Was she surprised he knew security agencies? Kinda. Though if she'd thought about it for half a millisecond, she wouldn't have been.

"Guest or working?"

"Both," she said and inhaled. "Oh, hey, his wife will be here! He's so neurotic about her safety."

"Says the woman who's supposed to be in love."

"Hey, when my guy feared for my safety, Stone's the guy he brought in to work with Ballard."

"Sean Ballard. Heard about him. Never met him."

Not far from Jane's shadow, Ballard was all about security in the transfer of guests and probably up to his eyeballs with concerns and potential issues. The man usually took a while to trust, but if Sam knew Ryder Stone and the Breckenridges, he might even be welcome to help. Hmm, that could've been something to bring up in the planning stage, if, you know, Sam made his whereabouts known.

"You can meet Ballard now if—" Hold up. "You want to meet our security chief before you meet the groom?"

"Not got a lot in common with a playboy billionaire, Talks-Alot."

"You assume," she said, fists finding her hips. "How do you know that? And he's not a playboy anymore, he's reformed."

"Just because I wasn't here, doesn't mean I wasn't watching."

"All you've seen is what the public see," she said. "What we are doesn't belong to them."

"Name one thing we have in common."

"He likes Scotch."

"I drink beer."

"He doesn't dance."

"He does with you."

Which Sam had flat out denied her. Damn. It had worked with Porter.

A-ha! "You both love me."

"Jury's out."

Stubborn jackass.

"Okay, you want to know who he is? He's the guy who has me surrounded by security every second of the day. And, yes, that includes the nighttime seconds. Just because they're not in the room, doesn't mean they aren't there.

"He's the guy who will, without ceremony or shame, send assistants scurrying around after me with cellphones, ensuring I have everything I want."

"Diva."

"And you know what I want every minute of every day?" Her palms landed on his waist. "Him, Sam. He's my best friend. You'll love him, I swear it. You can't know until you experience us. And not through a screen—"

"Okay, geez, you don't have to lay it on so thick. And you wonder why I stay away."

"I do wonder that," she said. "All your life, you've been trying to get away."

"I do my thing, you do yours," he said. "Sonia still with The Idiot?"

"God knows why…"

"You're one to talk."

"My husband is not an idiot." She laughed. "I don't know if I'll get used to that. *Husband.*"

"You're giddy, did the guy get you drunk or something?"

"Always before she gets out of bed," Zairn said, appearing around the column. She backed up a little when he came close to stroke her cheek. "People want to talk to you."

"I'm talking to people." She pointed at Sam. "Found this guy. And here we are… talking."

"Mm hmm."

The way he inspected her with such intensity was like he'd never seen her before, like there was no one else in the room. That adoration was appreciated, and they could get back to that… after she took a shot at surprising him.

"You'll like this one, I promise." He had no other choice. "Casanova," she said, filling her lungs. "Meet Samson Kyst. My brother."

TWENTY-FOUR

"NO KIDDING." Interest piqued, that revelation straightened Zairn up. "All this time I thought you were making him up."

"If I was, he'd be nicer."

"I won't call him that," Sam said, apparently forgetting Zairn could hear him.

"No, you don't call him that," she said, tucking herself against Zairn when he put an arm around her. "Only I call him that. He's Zairn or Z, whatever you prefer."

Zairn opened a hand, literally the hand of friendship, or maybe brotherhood. "Pleasure to finally meet you."

"He's not an idiot," she reassured her brother.

"Porter was an idiot."

"And maybe when you put on your big boy pants and bring someone home to us, we'll return the favor in passing judgment on your love matches. Just shake the guy's hand, geez, Sam."

Breathing in, he boosted his shoulder from the

pillar and shook hands with Zairn. God, she could've squealed in delight. Jane would've done it for her, if she'd been present.

"She'll drive you crazy," Sam said. "You've gotta watch her 'cause she gets mixed up in shit."

"I've noticed that about her." Zairn flashed her a smile. "I'm blessed she lets me ride along on her adventures."

"Most of the time you ride along."

"Most of the time," Zairn said in agreement. "Sam, you didn't sit up front with the family."

"That's not his style," she said, resisting the urge to loosen some buttons and slip a hand into Zairn's shirt. It had been too long since they'd been alone. "Sam is five years older than me. We were his annoying, sometimes flamboyant, younger sisters. I can be quite loud, and Sonia likes to perform. Sam stayed in the background. He's always been a background kind of guy. He's a watcher, not a doer."

"But you still asked me to dance with you."

"Well, you know, some might say it's a miracle I got down the aisle. Guess this is a 'stranger things have happened' kind of day."

"How long are you in town?" Zairn asked.

"A while."

See, just like she said, a 'stranger things have happened' day.

"You're staying in LA?" Could he tell that was just hilarious? The strained smile torturing her lips had to become a laugh. "You? In LA? For more than a minute?"

"Don't worry, you won't have to witness it."

"Oh, I will," she said, nodding vigorously. "I would not miss this for all the rubies in the world. My big brother in LA..." She patted his arm. "In the big, bright, shiny city. My awkward and uncomfortable big brother—"

"Don't you have a honeymoon to go on or something?"

"Nope, we did that already. And we're loaded, we can vacation whenever we want." She'd thought getting married or the wedding were supposed to be the highlights of her life. Sam, in LA, it would be like an SNL skit. "Did you bring your sunscreen?"

"I spend a lot of time around the equator."

"Ew, is that like a sex thing?"

Zairn squeezed her. "Since when do you ew at sex things?"

Her expression probably said it all. "Since they were coming out of my big brother's mouth."

"Is that how I get you to go away, Talks-Alot? Talk about sex?"

"Talks-A-Lot?" Zairn's amusement needed no translating. "That's what you call her? How come Blayne never told me that? Tells me everything else."

She coughed. "Didn't I tell you you're not allowed to talk to Blayne?"

"Why is he not allowed to talk to Blayne?" Sam asked.

Her regard flattened. "Would you want your other half talking to Blayne?"

"Good point," he said with the slightest nod before returning to his inspection of the room.

"Oh, oh…" She grabbed his hand, holding it in both of hers between them. "Does that mean there is another half? Do you have another half? Is that why you're here? Is she here?"

"Got a lot of potential targets in this room."

Tripp should be her next stop on Sam's introduction tour. Either they'd hit it off or hate each other's guts. Tripp never really hated anyone. Sam, on the other hand, found people distasteful. Not as individuals, just in general: people. And she called herself cynical? Where did it come from? Her big, beautiful brother, that's where.

"You haven't spoken to anyone in this room," Roxie said. "You can't fall in love with someone if you haven't spoken to them. What you're targeting is sex."

"What's wrong with that, Little Sister?"

"Nothing, but you can't sleep with anyone without talking to me first."

That brought not only his attention to her, but a slight lift of his upper lip. Was he laughing at her?

"I've gotta vet my dates through you?"

"Or Zairn," she said, completely serious.

"You're kidding me." Next time his scrutiny on the crowd seemed more intent. "Now I've gotta take one of these women home."

"You don't have a home," she said. "And you might be able to sleep with one, you just have to check with me first."

"Did you check with me before sleeping with him?" he asked, his chin bobbing in Zairn's direction.

"No, because you don't know him. I know all these people."

"Every single one? Your entire family consists of seven people… And Blayne's in the gray zone."

"Speaking of, I know you know men who own guns," she murmured, leaning in. "How come you haven't had any of them go all big-brotherly on Blayne yet?"

"He and Sonia deserve each other, Talks-A-Lot. I go big-brotherly when it's necessary. Besides…" Another nod at Zairn, "bet he knows some guys who own guns. Shit, you have access to Sean Ballard and Ryder Stone, what's the problem? Cost too much of your allowance?"

"They're on account, actually, and I instruct

them without Z's permission all the time."

"You do?" Zairn said like that was news to him.

It wasn't. The guy never got through saying that her access was absolute. And she did talk about these things, most of the time. Wasn't her fault if he chose not to listen.

"Might need the nod if you're paying them to kill a guy."

"You know, you're right though…" She sighed. "Blayne's not worth the potential charge. I like Ballard and Stone too much to send them to prison." Her head dropped against Zairn. "And this guy would be lost without me."

"Where do you think you're going?" Zairn asked. "We'll pin it on them. Tell the cops you were with me the whole time."

"I like this guy," Sam said, matter-of-fact.

She exaggerated her laugh. "Because he'll give me an alibi? Geez, brother, catch up to the now, please. Every time I get arrested, he bails me out or pulls strings. Z's got the routine down."

"Thought you knew she gets mixed up in shit."

"She does and I do," Zairn said. "I'm around to make sure she gets away with it."

Sam's eyes dropped to hers. "I like this guy."

Twice in as many minutes was a good sign.

"Well, too bad, he's taken," she said. "I already married him, find your own."

"He got a sister?"

"No, and ew again, you're not allowed to screw around in the family. Most of the women in this room are family, so I say again, check with me before you screw them."

"I know your rules."

"I know you know, but that's also not the point. A lot of these women are taken, occupied, otherwise involved with guys who don't like other guys moving in on their territory. Z knows everyone, he can hook you up with someone suitable. Someone unthreatening who won't get you maimed."

"He a pimp?"

"We've got to pay for the rubies somehow," she said. "But, no, though some woman here will owe him something, I'm sure one of them would take on a charity case like you. If not, we'll blackmail someone."

"Dark. Sinister… I like that."

"You're not really making the best impression on your new brother."

Zairn shrugged. "Hey, he likes me, my work is done."

"Good. Does that mean you won't speak to him on a regular basis like you do my dad?" She filled Sam in. "My Casanova actually likes talking to Dad. Freakish."

"Guess it's a different variety of acceptance when you grow up without one." That was—Sam said it so casually yet it was a tornado through her. "Right?"

"Nothing you can't find out on Huddle Hunt," Zairn responded to Sam, nonplussed.

Pushing away from her love to put her back to Sam, she reached up to her guy's jaw. "Why did you never tell me it like that?"

"It's not a big deal, Lo."

"It's a big deal. You can talk to my dad any time you want. All the time. He's your dad now too. Officially." Had been since last year but… "And you have a brother now. Another brother, a new brother, I know you have a lot of brothers. This one's not so easy to get on the phone. If you ever want to play a game of pin the tail on the hobo, he's good to chase around the planet. Don't expect to find him though, so keep your wagers low."

"Hobo?" Sam asked.

"What? You're homeless, aren't you? Of no fixed abode? It's just another word for drifter."

"But you chose to go the shabby way."

She shrugged. "It's a choice. Same as your choice to float around the world like abandoned litter. You know you're not twenty-two anymore, brother, right?"

"Roxanna is good at keeping tabs on her people," Zairn said. "Always surprised me you were the exception. Family is important to her."

Both of the blood and non-blood variety.

"It's not through lack of trying, I'll give her that."

"Yeah, Sam suits himself, comes and goes. Of course…" Facing her brother again, she rested back against Zairn. "If you'd stayed in touch, you'd be living the billionaire lifestyle right now."

"I'll pass, thanks."

"Always on the move. Keeping to himself. Mr. Lone Wolf."

"We move in different circles, Talks-A-Lot."

"It's like we're from different planets. Are you sure we came from the same womb?"

"Objectively…" Zairn said, which immediately piqued her radar.

Her acuity narrowed. "Objectively what? Hmm, Skippy? Remember you want to get laid tonight."

"Babe, it's only fair to highlight, we don't stick in the one place for too long either."

"Yeah, maybe these days I travel, but it's not like in my blood…" Though maybe Sam was proof that vagrancy was in the genes. "And I have a fixed abode. I'm contactable."

"If Astrid charges your phone."

"I'm really surprised you've chosen abstinence on your wedding night, Skippy."

But her love laughed and wrapped both arms around her shoulders. "Until you remember I'm so good at it."

"This isn't a conversation I want to witness."

What? They were just standing there, together, against each other, thinking about… The "so good at it" thing might mean something to them, but it was pretty easy to place what they were talking about. If Sam was the one in her place with his own partner… Yeah, moving on.

"Casanova, you'll never guess what, Sam's a Ballard fanboy."

"Really? Don't get many of those."

Hmm, not entirely accurate. "Male fans might be few and far between, maybe, but women love the growling. Ballard's good at the growling. Not as good as some, but… Sam knows Ryder too."

"Then he has good taste in friends," Zairn said. "Worked together?"

Sam's head tilted. "What is it you think I do?"

"You'd be more likely to get an answer from Ryder on that," Roxie said. "We can introduce Sam to Ballard though, maybe he could use a hand."

"Tonight? You want your brother to work at our wedding?"

"Your best man is working. My best friend, in addition to getting married herself, is working." She swept her arm in front of her, though the majority of the room and the guests were behind Zairn, the support at her back. "And this, talking to people, schmoozing, hosting, smiling at the masses, is a huge part of what we do on a daily basis."

Huh, good point, she hadn't put those pieces together like that until right then. It was so routine, it was completely natural.

"You were right about the getting married again," Zairn said, more serious than before. Skippy rearing his head? "Next time we'll do it the way you want."

"You didn't want this?" Sam asked.

"I did! I do! I've had an excellent day. Jane's purview is exactly what I wanted. Z's a go-getter, that's what it is, he doesn't like to be beaten. Everything's a competition, even with himself. Always likes to think we can aim higher."

That wasn't why the suggestion came up though. Playing up to the image, the public perception, was necessary sometimes.

Knowing him, like she did, that wasn't one-upmanship talking. No, her Casanova was pissed at himself. He pushed himself harder than anyone else.

"You said intimate," Zairn said, "don't think I forgot."

"This day has been wonderful, perfect." She pushed the crown of her head against him. "Intimate comes later."

"I don't need to be standing here for this," Sam said.

She and Zairn talked about sex a lot. Hmm. Maybe she'd have pegged that. It wasn't until her brother was right there pointing it out that she considered it may not be a normal thing to do around people. That was her girls' fault too though. All of them had sex on the brain. Worked out for their guys, so who was complaining? No one else would go around correcting them, that was for sure.

Her brother was a grouch, plain and simple, that didn't mean she couldn't take a shot at lightening him up. Something she'd been doing since they were kids. He'd call it pestering, she liked to think of it more as a public service. God help any woman interested in getting with the grump.

"You know, you're right," she said, biting the corner of her lip. One way to ease his load would be to help him… eject that load, as it were. "Scroogey, we need to get Sam a girl."

"You don't," her brother said. "I get my own girls."

Didn't look like he was doing a bang-up job of it, standing there at the edge of the pack making a point of distancing himself.

"Zairn would've said that once too, then fate delivered me to him. Stroke of luck. That's me. I can be your stroke of luck. Just call me Cupid."

"Please, don't tax yourself," he said, monotone.

"Are you coming to the club?"

"Haven't decided."

"I'd say you can fly in the chopper with us, but you'd be disappointed to miss a chance to rappel from the thing."

"If there's a chance for that kind of fun, I'll go upstairs and grab my kit."

Oh, so predictable, though still entertaining. "Doesn't surprise me you carry that kind of thing as standard. Does surprise me you'd stay in a place like this. Did you find some janitor's closet big enough for your sleeping bag and just set up shop?"

"That's the thing, Talks-A-Lot, sometimes a guy has to be comfortable in comfort, even when he prefers the dirt."

Something about that statement sparked a thought.

"We need to dig up Kinloch," she muttered over her shoulder to her guy.

Sam got the reference. "Kinloch Peake, I've spent time on his land."

"Of course you have."

Because Sam spent most of his life trying to make sure he never slept in one place twice. That meant spreading himself out… a lot.

"He has a lot of it," Zairn said. "More soon."

"With all the wealth he's just acquired—"

"Man's always had a lot of wealth from how I hear it," Sam said. "Got a lot of respect for a guy dedicated to the land like that. He might be the only loaded guy I have a chance of understanding."

"Well, I'm so sorry, he's not my type," she said. "Whoever marries him will probably have to live in a cave."

That amused her leaning post. "That's funny because it's probably true."

"Guy might surprise you."

Or not. "A lot of people were surprised by Kinloch's decision to sell his family's life work," she said. "Got to admit, I don't know him too well, but even I was surprised. Maybe if I'd thought about if from the point of view of a guy like you…"

"Don't know a better use for money."

"Than to buy isolation? That's exactly what you'd do if we gave you a charge card, isn't it?"

"No, I'd shove the thing up your ass," Sam said, clearly annoyed. "You were never about the money, Talks-Alot."

Porter noted that about her too, once upon a time. These days, it frustrated her when people looked at Zairn and only saw money. When those people assumed he was shallow and arrogant. Okay, so his ego wasn't lacking, but none of that was the sum total of him. She liked being the one who saw him at his most unguarded, his most honest. That didn't mean she wanted those she loved to believe any of the assumptions in the press.

Zairn pounced to her defense. "She still isn't."

Sigh, it was nice while it lasted. They'd gotten along for… oh, at least three minutes.

"What happened to you liking each other?"

"I like him so long as he shows you respect,"

Zairn said, with a hard edge she'd heard in his voice before, usually with people he considered harmful to her or them. "This is her wedding day."

"Don't care," Sam said. "She deserves respect every day. As long as you're good for her, I'll keep the peace. Minute I think you're not… don't forget I'm watching."

"From so far away, you haven't seen her the whole time I've known her. I've had a chance to learn her, love her, and have her love me, and you haven't shown up once."

"Still watching."

"Okay, everyone, this is a happy day. Happy times. Happy faces. I love both of you and you love me. This is family. We're family. We'll go to the club, get drunk, make some memories."

"Heard a rumor you have a skit."

Her brother often managed to hear rumors. Always surprised her given she never saw him talking to anyone. Who exactly was sharing these rumors? Insect life? Rodents? Couldn't be the homo sapiens.

"A skit?" she asked.

"A musical number."

Ah, her birthday. Good times.

"Come to the club and maybe you'll get a front row seat."

No, there weren't really seats. Maybe she should pull him up on stage, just to guarantee his excellent view. Funny that while she'd be performing, being ridiculous for hundreds of viewers, Sam would be the more mortified one up there. Had never been his thing, being the center of attention. Probably why she and Sonia excelled at it.

"Hmm," he pondered. "Not sure that's a good deal. I've heard you sing."

"By the time I get up there, you'll be too drunk

to care. Besides, what do you think autotune is for?" she asked and snagged his hand again. "We'll find Ballard, you can buddy up, and maybe you'll have a good time."

"Maybe."

"It's a risk you have to take," she said, beaming. "It's my wedding day. You can't say no."

TWENTY-FIVE

MOST EVERYONE HAD been transported to the club. Two thirds of people at least, she'd guess. Jane and Knox went on ahead to settle their guests at Crimson while she and Zairn stayed behind to balance out festivities. After checking with them, staff shut three of the quadrants to begin cleaning up. A task she didn't envy them.

Zairn was somewhere, could be at the club already, or upstairs sleeping it off, no idea. Okay, he wouldn't be sleeping it off because this was Zairn Lomond. He could be upstairs taking the edge off, but if that was the case why was she down there?

She smiled. Nodded at this person and that. Maybe she should go upstairs and text her guy to follow. Wouldn't be the first time they'd ditched a party at their club being thrown in their honor... with a free bar, however that worked out. Shame this was a no phone day. Could end up being a no phone month because she had no idea where hers had landed.

Mieux emerged from the guests, making a

beeline for her. Ah, a friend.

"Hey, honey," she said, raising an arm as Mieux rushed over. "I haven't seen you yet. I haven't seen anyone, I don't even know if Zairn's still here. Do you know if Zairn's still here?"

Hmm, losing her husband so soon after the ceremony was sort of careless.

"We have a problem," Mieux said, ignoring the invitation to hug.

"Okay." In the subtle, sexy cocktail dress, Mieux was positively delicious. Something she'd always known about the beauty. It wasn't much like the usually work focused Mieux to let loose and she liked it. "You know you're not working, right? You shouldn't be working."

A lot of people were working. What fabulous employers they were turning out to be. "Please come to our wedding and work for no pay." They wouldn't get away with doing this more than once. No one would show up a second time.

"Uh huh." Mieux took her arm to pull her through people to the side of the room. "We have a problem. Tripp is trying to contain that problem but…"

"A problem?"

One that required her and not her husband? Many preferred coming to her about non-businessy things. Because she was more approachable? Because Zairn had better things to do? Because she wasn't a defer kind of woman?

More than likely it was because Zairn didn't always care that much about "problems." They never raised his blood pressure. Some of that nonchalance rubbed off on her too, but she at least let people be heard.

"Definitely a problem."

"Where are we—"

In a shadowy corner, behind the pillar that had

been Sam's, Mieux put her back to the wall and held up a device. A video or live feed of the woman who'd stunk out press not so long ago claiming to be Zairn's mistress: Anjelica.

"It's only right I be allowed in there," the beauty claimed on-screen. "Crimson is as much mine as it is hers."

Crimson… There were so many people crowded around in the background, there wasn't much view of the street.

"Where is she?"

"Outside the club. Crimson, LA," Mieux murmured. "Right now. This is happening as we speak."

Oh, brother.

Drama. There would need to be a lot of sex if they ever wanted to level this seesaw.

Anjelica wasn't done. "If I was there, at the hotel, in there, he would've seen me and—she's jealous. She knows he'd pick me over her."

Huh, maybe this wasn't what she'd thought it was after all.

"I'm the bad guy?" she asked Mieux, not mad or offended, just clarifying she had it straight. "I'm the bad guy. Okay."

Shining from the screen, the woman at the center of her view was beautiful and people were interested, crowding up close, maybe trying to listen. Either Anjelica had fans or the cohort wanted to be on camera. There were usually at least a few of those folk as soon as the lens rose. Not that she could judge, she had her own damn lens, many of them, and didn't shy from glittering in front of them.

"What do you want to do?" Mieux asked. "Security? Salad?"

"No! God, no," she said. "That gives her words so much more weight. We ignore it."

"Ignore it?"

"Ignored it the first time."

"Didn't Zairn want to say something the first time? It's horrible. I can't believe he would—"

"We don't dignify it." Their reaction would get more press than one woman making unsubstantiated claims. "Where's Tripp?"

"At the club."

"Tell him to keep his ass there, and to stay out of the fire. Just because there's a beautiful woman in the mix does not mean he has to mobilize," Roxie said, taking the tablet as Mieux retrieved her phone from a pocket.

A pocket! On a dress like that? She should be buying custom.

"He's your friend."

"I know he means well…" Didn't people always? Intentions. Path. That kind of thing. "But she could be his future wife for all we know. It's better that we don't acknowledge it, don't give it our airtime."

Especially on that day of all days.

"We don't dignify it?"

"Exactly."

With that clarification, Mieux put the phone to her ear, going a little away to talk to Tripp.

The device grabbed her attention again.

"All these people out here…" Anjelica spoke louder, over the din of the masses. No one was shouting, as such, the noise just came with the volume of the interested community. Maybe hosting their après reception in a city club hadn't been the best idea. "They're here because they love him."

"If he wanted you in there, why weren't you invited?" someone asked off-screen.

From behind the camera? Was the speaker the one holding the lens or just some random in the crowd?

"She would never let that happen," Anjelica said, raising her chin. "She controls him. Everything about him."

"'Cept where he sticks his dick if we're to believe you." High score to the heckler. "Which is it?"

Raising the screen, she increased the volume. "Wait…"

Did she recognize that voice?

"She manipulates him," Anjelica continued. "He's sweet and passionate, she takes advantage of his kind heart."

"And you would never do that?" the cynic asked. "Take advantage of Zairn Lomond or the media, to increase your own visibility?"

As much as Anjelica faltered, she didn't lose her confidence. "This isn't about my visibility, it's about supporting the man I love."

"You can claim to love him, that's your feelings. You can't speak to his though. The Zairn Lomond I know is tough, assertive, fair. If he loved you, why would he marry Roxie?"

"Because she knows things. She blackmails him."

"Into marrying her?" The scoff of laughter was—she did know that voice! "Must be some serious dirt."

Her posture righted. "Reeve Crosby."

Why would he…?

"Zairn loves me," Anjelica asserted. "It's complicated. I should be allowed to speak to him, to see him, to be with him."

"Because you claim something you can't substantiate? When did you meet? How long was your affair? When was the last time you spent the night with him? Or is it just sex and he leaves money on the nightstand?"

Oh, ouch, that was vicious. At least he didn't

reserve his question volley technique specifically for her. And it worked too. Without any need for Anjelica's retort, Reeve had put doubt in the listeners' mind. She'd like to think that doubt was already there, but few knew Zairn the way his inner circle did.

"I am not—I don't care about his money! I love him!"

"When was the last time you talked?" Reeve asked. "If this wedding is happening against his will, he must've called you today."

"He did! He did call me."

"That's funny because he specifically told his assistant that he wasn't taking any calls today."

"It was before—"

"From the moment he woke up."

"He would never—"

"Because he wasn't allowed to talk to Roxie before the wedding, he said he wouldn't be speaking to anyone."

How did Reeve Crosby know that? She hadn't even known that, but it was something her guy would be likely to do. If he couldn't have her, he wouldn't have anyone.

"He has a phone just for me."

"That his assistant has never seen?"

"How do you—this isn't about you!" Anjelica was getting riled. "You don't understand our relationship."

"Because you've yet to give details. Where did you meet?"

One beat. Another. Was Anjelica trying to decide whether to answer or pondering which lie to tell?

"We met at his club."

"Which one?" Reeve asked.

"In… here. This one."

"LA? And when was the last time you saw him,

in person?"

"Last night."

"He had a bachelor party last night."

"After," Anjelica said. "We met after his party."

Wow, so Zairn squeezed Anjelica in between leaving his party and screwing his wife in the Platinum Suite? Must've been one helluvan elevator ride. Casanova would get a talking to for that. She'd suggested Grand Hotel elevator sex the night they got married. He hadn't followed through with her, but instead used her idea with his hussy?

Zairn hadn't seen this. Who would show it to him? A brave soul. It would only frustrate him. He didn't like it when their love was brought into question, when his dedication to her was doubted. Not in such a specific, explicit way. Wasn't one of her most loved moments either, but it had to be left in perspective.

"Who is this guy? Your director?" Reeve asked and the camera moved. "Did you come out to film yourself here? The world won't feel sorry for you. Some think you were setup, that you're being taken advantage of to paint Zairn or Roxie in a bad light."

"I am here because I want to be, because I have to be."

"It wasn't some impulse or a deep-seated drive. You took the time to do hair, makeup—and why didn't you go to the hotel?"

"I tried!" Anjelica called, dampness rimming her eyes. "I went there and they wouldn't let me in."

"They wouldn't let you in at the hotel, so you thought they'd let you in here? Look around you, plenty of crazies had the same idea."

"I am not crazy! He loves me!"

"He loves Lola!" someone in the crowd called out.

"Everyone loves Lola!" came another voice.

Well, that was nice. Who didn't like love? At least one, rather two, particular people liked her. Was it only them who—

The crowd chanted. It started slow and… She tipped her head to hear the name in two sure syllables.

"Lo-la, Lo-la."

Curling her lips around her teeth, the flattery wanted her to laugh, though it was absurd, but it was… Those people…

Anjelica seemed to be talking, her lips were moving, but the crowd drowned her out.

"Rox…" Mieux approached again. "Do you hear—"

"I hear it."

Maybe if they went to the street, they'd hear it vibrate through the city.

Mieux was just as astounded. "I've never…"

"When we get to the club," Roxie said, "bring him upstairs."

"Him?"

"Reeve Crosby. I want to speak to him alone in our pod."

The chant grew in volume and ferocity. Yet another reason she and Zairn didn't need to involve themselves. The people had their backs. Their people. As much as anyone in their employ, those people on the street were theirs too.

They'd gathered without invitation, knowing the club was closed, just on the chance of catching a glimpse. These were their people and they answered Anjelica's accusations themselves. Zairn loved her, only her, and none of those incredible individuals would hear any different.

TWENTY-SIX

ZAIRN WAS ALREADY on the roof when someone came to tell her it was time to go. With the rotors going, and an audience, they didn't have time to talk. Not that there was anything to say. He may not be aware of the Anjelica thing at all.

At the club, they were whisked into a sea of people. They'd used the main dance floor for her birthday celebration. That night was access all areas. Their guests took up space upstairs, downstairs, and in the VIP suite, anywhere they wanted.

She had an appointment, so as Zairn was coopted by a bunch of unknown suits—that wasn't a fair descriptor, practically every guy there wore a suit—she headed for their base. Zairn had a preferred private pod in LA's Crimson. It had been his preferred space before her too, a lot happened in that room, but it was a place she didn't mind setting as off-limits.

Mieux was the one she'd sent on the mission, but it was Stephen Barrow who opened the door to let Reeve Crosby inside.

"Want me to stay?" Stephen asked, eyeing Crosby like he wasn't best pleased with the reporter.

"No, but don't go far." He started to leave. "But, hey, where have you been these last two weeks?"

"Here," Stephen said. "Someone had to run the show with Ballard in New York."

She liked that. How their family pitched and heaved and got things done.

"We've come a long way, Riot Guy. And to think one day you sent me to jail."

His smile was lopsided. "Night's still young, Kyst."

As he slipped out, she just shook her head. What a world they lived in. But he was right, with her, and LA, there was always a chance of civil unrest and law enforcement intervention. They were kind of already halfway there.

"You rang?" Crosby said.

Not literally, but, yeah. "You want a drink?" she asked, going to the wall panel to adjust the lighting and the music.

She wanted somewhere quiet to talk, didn't want to miss the party entirely. And a hostess knew how important ambiance was to getting what she wanted.

"Didn't you get married today?"

"I did." She glanced back. "Sit down."

"And I'm here for... This gonna be like a piñata thing?"

"Are piñatas standard at weddings? We haven't had one yet."

"I meant—"

"I know what you meant."

With everything in order, she stepped out of her ruby slippers and headed to the drink awaiting her on the table. Even on their wedding day, surrounded by friends, her drink monitor loitered on the other side of the glass, fixated on her drink.

"Shoes are a nice touch."

"I thought so."

"Like the hair too."

"Thank you." She dropped onto the couch, right in the middle. A novelty. She didn't usually have the thing to herself. "Are you going to sit down?"

"I assume we're waiting for someone."

"Are we?" She sipped her drink and crossed her legs, bundling them onto the couch next to her. "Who? I didn't know you had a plus one."

"You have a plus one."

"I don't know where he is right now." She relaxed against the backrest. "And you probably don't want him to join us."

"Why not?"

"Because his last experience with you involved a security bailout." Short memory. "I don't know that he knows what happened tonight."

He chose a perpendicular armchair. "You really haven't talked to him?"

"I said that, didn't I?"

"So why am I here?"

"Everything, this entire conversation, is off the record." After his nod, she continued. "I know what happened tonight. And unless it was some elaborate ruse, you did good."

"Thank you."

She leaned close to whisper, "Was it an elaborate ruse?"

Glaring, the question didn't amuse. "No."

"Why speak out?"

His mouth opened a little, he breathed, pondering? Checking himself? Did he plan to hold back or let rip?

"You are a human being, Roxie, and this is your

wedding day. Do I think Zairn's squeaky-fucking-clean? No, I don't. But…"

Five second wait. Ten seconds. Was she supposed to say something? What was he expecting? She needed more information before making a move.

"Go on," she said in her best patient, understanding therapist voice.

"There were things on the tablet…"

"Bad things? Incriminating things? Angry things? Dick pics? Homemade porn? Oh, are you a plushie?"

Didn't he just get a thousand times more interesting!

The line of his lips thinned, except this time he wasn't annoyed, he almost seemed… amused. Another person who thought she was crazy. Damn, why not own it?

"Things that might've been of interest to you."

"Things I'd be mad at if I read them?" She touched the surface of her drink. "I meant what I said. Zairn's the one you have to thank for that. He's the voice of reason in a lot of rooms."

"And that forty-eight-hour period was…" His inhale came with a head shake. "Is that how you live every day?" Ah, a little empathy, perhaps. "Waiting for someone to broadcast your biggest secret?"

"Unfortunately for the press, I don't have any big secrets. I barely have any little ones."

"If that's true, why surround yourself with security?"

"Security is less about the media and more about the fanatics." That wasn't fair. "Sometimes, if we're out and about, people crowd close, and they could get hurt. Security is there to keep people safe, not hide some dark secret."

"You restrict access."

"I don't know any public figure who doesn't. We

can't have an open door, 'come on over and watch us eat' policy. Sometimes we have to shower and sleep."

"You're entitled to privacy."

"Wow," she said. "Can I have that in writing?"

"I stand by what I said, you're a celebrity and people want to get close. You're living the dream."

"One you know more about than you let on. How did you know what you said outside to Anjelica? About Zairn and his assistant?"

"Think you've got a mole?"

"In Tibbs? No." Was Hell getting chilly? "I probably should've checked it was true before asking you."

"If it was true? Zairn didn't tell you about the phone?"

"I didn't speak to him this morning, that was true. And don't change the subject, tell me how you knew."

"Tibbs."

"It was not Tibbs." She breathed out. "You were eavesdropping or someone was. Hotel staff?"

As far as she knew, her guy hadn't left the hotel, so it would have to be someone with access to the suite.

"Maybe…"

And that sly expression intrigued.

It hit her. "The butler," she said. "Damnit."

Zairn probably hadn't had the chance to tell the guy to take a hike. She'd been staying in that suite for a couple of weeks, it had almost become a home from home. Usually, their lives were protected, their privacy secure. Her guy's rules should stand whether he was around or not. Lesson learned.

"I don't give up my sources."

"No, of course not."

"The guy loses his job and I'll—"

"We don't go around firing people, or

demanding they be fired." They could demand certain people not be in their vicinity though. Preserving their privacy was important. "It is what it is."

"Reasoned," he said. "Will your husband agree with you?"

"I don't know, ask Anjelica, apparently I make all the decisions and manipulate him, blackmail him." The tapering of his eyes zeroed in, he tilted his head, suggesting confusion. "What is it? Come on. Just say it. This is a safe space."

"Ha, if only that was true."

"It is, for the duration of this conversation," she said. "I've had enough champagne to loosen up the boundaries." Her head dropped to the side as she whispered. "Just don't tell Z."

"You don't seem like that, like you'd manipulate him. Maybe you do. From my experience you're less… subtle."

Blunt was one of Zairn's favorite words for her. Thanks, Knox. Manipulation did take time and effort she'd rather not waste. And if they couldn't be honest with each other…

She chose to take that observation as a compliment. "Thank you."

"When it comes to the press… He's much more relaxed with us now than he was before you."

"And…"

"And explain it to me. I don't—everything Anjelica says, you say it's a lie."

"It is."

"So how do you sit here, smiling, living your life without… Why don't you speak out? Tell the truth. Tell the people the truth, whatever it is."

"Defend my relationship? My husband? My honor?"

"Yes!"

On a head shake, she laughed. "To who? I love him and he loves me. We have a life together, communication, respect… My life is incredible and I've never been happier. What difference does it make what a stranger says to the press? Saying it doesn't make it true."

"But your stream, the clubs, and—"

"Business is fine. And I talk to people through my streams, sometimes I answer questions. I'm always honest. I'll tell the truth or decline to talk about something if it crosses a line. Anjelica, she… either she's a plant or she's sick. Z and I are more likely to help her get help than think about tearing her down. There's no satisfaction in that."

"People doubt, when you stay quiet, they think there's a story."

"Is that what you think? Okay…" She righted her dress over her knee. "Let's say it's true, that everything the faux mistress is saying is true." No juicy quote in that. "Hypothetically."

"Yeah…"

"That's a conversation I would have with my partner. Even if we broke up, I wouldn't go crying to the press, it makes no sense. There's no validation in that for me. So knowing it's not true, it's barely worth a conversation with Zairn, why would it warrant one with Anjelica or the mass media?"

"You're just cool with it?"

Her lips curled. "It's today and tomorrow will be tomorrow. There are real, honest to God problems in the world that should upset all of us. Someone lies about Zairn today and someone else lies about me tomorrow, it never ends. We take a deep breath and appreciate what's real."

"Your relationship?"

"Yes."

"Because you love him?"

"Yes."

"And you're sure he's not cheating on you?"

"Yes."

Beyond her drink observer, Sam stood by one of the VIP bars. Nice. Glad he'd come.

"I don't think many people would be this understanding."

"The world wants a cat fight," she said. "And I won't dignify it. Anjelica can shout and scream and stamp her feet. Nothing she says will impact my relationship or my happiness."

"I can't decide if…"

"I have the healthiest relationship in the world or I'm the most naïve woman on the planet?"

More amusement. "Right."

"I get that a lot."

Her brother wasn't alone. For once. Rather than be on the edge looking in, he was talking, animated, not as entirely grumpy as she might expect.

"What…?" Reeve's head turned as he followed her line of sight. "Is there a problem?"

"No," she murmured. "I just feel like that guy should be familiar."

Not her brother, the guy standing next to him, in their little cluster. Her brother didn't cluster. He didn't socialize, not like the rest of the world did.

"This is your reception, shouldn't you know everyone?"

She scoffed. "You might think so, but…"

"Don't know the guy in the middle, but the guy with the red rose on his lapel is Ridge Wylde." She mouthed the name. Good thing someone knew what was what. "Rose is an odd touch. He can't have been in the wedding party."

Because otherwise she really should know him.

That was one answer she could give. "It's a Crimson rose. They were handed out as people arrived. Party favors."

"I didn't get one."

"You didn't come through the front door," she said. And he wasn't an official guest. Was the guy's name supposed to mean something to her? "Am I meant to know Ridge Wylde?"

"He has a TV show."

"Oh, a celebrity."

"You might've seen his face here and there."

Why would her brother be talking to a celebrity? He didn't care about fame. Maybe, like her, he had no idea what the guy did for a living.

People were more than the sum total of their jobs. She was. Her guy was. Their friends. Their—what would Sam have in common with a TV star?

Curiosity piqued.

"There's a lot of pretty people around here," she muttered.

"That's LA for you."

All the pretty people. The city was rife with contradictions. Massive wealth juxtaposed with crippling poverty. Some cities had their own personality, their own attitude. After growing up in Chicago, she had to admit that New York was more her pizzazz. It had panache, its own style.

California wasn't as familiar. She liked it, but the money meant more there. No one could deny New York had prosperity. Wall Street, Park Avenue, hello! But in LA, they wore their successes, enhanced them, begged anyone to challenge them. Though when someone did, which did happen, there wasn't the same front they'd get from Chicago and New York. People were more sensitive, maybe that was it.

Reeve cleared his throat. "Can we talk about the

last minute twist?"

"What last minute twist?"

"I heard Knox Collier got married too. To your best friend. Is it true?"

"Might be."

"All that goodwill for the Anjelica thing over already?"

"You didn't do it for goodwill. Maybe you did, but it's my wedding day, so I choose not to be cynical." For once. "If Knox Collier, and/or my best friend have news to share, it's their news to share. Or not. What about you?"

"I didn't get married today."

Ha, funny. "Maybe not, but is there a special someone?"

Had she seen evidence of a significant other at his apartment? Not that she remembered, though she hadn't really been looking.

"Are we friends now?"

The door behind her, the one they'd entered by, opened, swiveling her all the way around and putting Reeve on his feet.

No one should've been able to open that door except—

"Ah, my husband," she said on a sigh, arms falling open.

TWENTY-SEVEN

IN A BLINK, the walls of the private pod went black. Dyce glass. Had its moments.

"Great!" she exclaimed with her own level of sarcasm. "Now people will think we're having a threesome in here."

Said husband wasn't in the mood to play. "They won't because he's leaving. Now."

"Don't be rude to our guest, I invited him."

"I know. He's still leaving."

Reeve tried to reason. "Zairn—"

"Don't talk to me like you're my friend. The only reason you get me and not security is because my wife's in a good mood."

His wife. Wow. Just wow. Still weird but goddamn sexy.

"Okay, everyone…" Much as it pained her—because she was tired and scrunchy and just wanted to cuddle—she forced herself to put one foot on the floor then the other. Yes, she could play mediator… or they'd die of laughter while she tried. "No fisticuffs on wedding days."

No doubt it was always someone's wedding day somewhere. Still not a bad ambition.

"Rox—"

"Thank you for speaking with me, Reeve, I appreciate your time."

Zairn opened the door and there was security, ready and prepped to "escort" him out. Politely, of course… she hoped.

"Go," Zairn said.

"I'll call you," Roxie said.

The reporter was dubious. "You'll call?"

"Yes," she said. "Some time. Eventually."

She wouldn't make any promises when this was kind of an unusual time. Weddings. Marriage. All that zest and zazz.

Reeve muttered something before being swept outside by security. The door closed as a final period to their meeting.

"Roxanna—"

"Ah! Ah! Ah!" she rebuked, wagging a finger. "It's our wedding day. That means you can't start an argument with me and I can't tell you off for rudely excusing my friends."

"Friend? Reeve Crosby is not our friend, babe."

"Okay." Extending her arms, she curled her fingers in and out of her palms, gesturing for him. "Come make-out with me."

Now they were alone, anyone paying attention might believe they were enjoying some married couple time. Who was she to disappoint them?

"That why you had Reeve Crosby in here?"

"Oh, yeah, 'cause he's totally my type. He doesn't have a skyscraper penthouse."

When he reached her, she let her hands slide across his body and around until she was holding herself against him. There in that space…

"You wouldn't look at me," she murmured, eyes closed. "One year ago today…"

"Lo…"

"*Something you can't get from me.*"

Those were his words that night. Missing it was the biggest mistake of her life, her biggest regret. That night, this man couldn't put his arms around her. And there, on their wedding day, he embraced her like she was the most precious thing in his world.

"I was blind."

"Lola—"

"We've been over this, I know, yet I haven't gotten the truth out, let me…"

Words were her style, she always had something to say, a phrase for any occasion. Except it didn't matter how many times they'd touched on the issue, she'd never managed to articulate what had been inside her back then.

"You can have anything you want," he murmured, tucking a tendril of hair behind her ear.

Language neglected her. And when he said that… there was only one thing she wanted…

"Kiss me, Casanova."

No explanation or justification needed. Bleeding satisfaction, he ducked to rest his mouth on hers. Was there such a thing as too much happiness, too much love? Their lives could follow any path. Up, down, it didn't matter. Left, right, they'd figure it out.

Fisting her hands in his shirt, she maneuvered them onto the couch, their lips never parting, and climbed on top, still holding him steady. When his fingers curled in her hair, she laid her palms flat to put just enough space between them to talk.

"I love you, Casanova. This is it now. Our forever." Pressing a little harder, she met his eye, appreciating the solid anchor of his chest and the beat of his strong heart. "You are one half of me. No other woman will ever touch you like this. No other person will ever match our entitlement to each other. Do you understand that?"

"I understand." His hands skimmed across her face, went into her hair, to her shoulders, he just, appreciated her. "I will never want another person."

Some may roll their eyes, some may speculate about who they may meet one day. She wasn't sure she understood it herself, not completely, but just the idea of him touching another woman the way he touched her was utterly ludicrous.

"There's no out from here," she said. "We will make this work. We will rely on each other. We'll respect our trust. I trust you."

"And I'd never abuse that trust."

The tender scrutiny of his eyes matched the lazy smile that occupied his neglected lips. She kissed him again, just because she could.

"We will never, ever forget to communicate." The words slid from her tongue to his as she whispered them against him. "There's nothing we can't say to each other. We tell the truth."

"No matter what it is. Agreed."

"We'll never rush to judgment. We stay calm. And we don't get mad at each other for telling the truth, we talk it out." His thumb grazed her lower lip. "You're giving me the 'you're crazy' look again."

"You're unique," he said. "Do things in your own time. Don't let anyone rush you." Except herself. "I love you."

"Doesn't explain the look." Not entirely. "Haven't you always known those things about me?"

He cupped her face, holding her near. "This is the conversation I wanted to have a year ago."

Ah, okay. "I'm sorry for the Triple Seven."

"Accepted. We're past that. I wanted to rush and you paced us. I wouldn't want to have this conversation unless you were ready for it. I should thank you."

"Thank me?"

"You didn't have this conversation until you were ready. Sure. We bypassed so much bullshit by waiting until this was guaranteed. You could've sprinted in, a lot of women would have. We could've had months of back and forth, together, apart, fighting, resisting, pushing, demanding. When you weren't sure, you kept your distance. And the minute you were…"

"The moment it hit me, I knew I'd do anything. I'd still do anything."

"There's nothing to do, we're here now. Neither of us have doubts. Our foundation, the way we came together, gave us that. We can speak on behalf of each other, voice certainty about our fidelity because we have honesty."

"Because we communicate." She nudged her face against his cheek. "Not bad for a lunatic charlatan, huh?"

"You're my lunatic charlatan, Lola. All I want is the complete, unfiltered you."

"Hmm, I know your game…" she teased, her teeth dragging on his jaw. "Stop thinking about sleeping with me."

"Can't help myself."

She pressured her palms up to his shoulders and trailed her fingertips back down to unfasten his shirt.

"In the name of honesty, there's something I have to tell you," she breathed, resting her cheek on his so her lips were near his ear. "I've been meaning to tell you for a while."

His own touch demanded more, stroking and caressing until his hands were beneath the fabric squeezing her ass.

"What's that?" he asked, his voice dropping an octave.

"I'm ready now."

"Ready for…?"

Leaning back, she wiggled her finger in front of his face, showing off the Empress ruby. "I'm ready."

He exhaled a laugh. "It's about goddamn time."

With a kiss they sealed the moment and their union. Together was an abstract concept until they found each other. Forever meant less. Now, an eternity wasn't long enough for Lola and Casanova.

EPILOGUE

LYING SIDE BY SIDE, facing each other, their mouths had been joined for… ever.

"How many days have we been here?" she whispered.

His fingertips trailed from her temple, sweeping aside tendrils of hair. "Not enough."

That had been his answer the last few times the sun peeked over the horizon. Light barely made it around the blackout curtains Zairn demanded in all their suites, wherever they were in the world.

No calls. No one in sight. When they wanted food, Zairn used the hotel app to request room service, which was left at the suite door. Never another soul in sight. Everything they needed whenever they needed it. And at the top of that list…

"One more day," she whispered. "I'll always want one more day with you all to myself."

"You'll always get it."

The world still turned. Whatever was going on out there, Zairn didn't want them to know. She'd said he could charge his phone. That he could meet if people needed him. And his reply every time: "You get me all to yourself."

"Feels like we just met," she murmured.

"Every moment with you is new. I live them like they're the first."

And last. Because this had to be bliss. Any heavenly paradise wouldn't beat this. Unless it meant never parting to eat or shower… okay, so they'd been doing even those together too.

"Think the world is worried?"

"I don't care about the world." The deft, light touch of his fingers awoke so much more than her heart. "I got all I need right here."

"Rouge needs you."

"You want to get out of here?" he asked, teasing her with another soft kiss.

Everything in her wanted to exist there. Only there. "Better call Hatfield, tell him Roxiverse won't happen."

"It can happen."

"Always knew I'd get my cheap porno life out of our relationship."

Zairn's mouth just grazed hers. "That beach sounds like a fine place to be right now."

"Jane and Knox have Crimson Isle all to themselves."

That island had a lot to answer for in Jane and Knox's relationship. Agreeing to cut that place off from the rest of the world was the least they could do for their best friends. Call it a wedding present no one else could give.

The where mattered less to them than it might to others. LA was special to their relationship, a lot of places meant something to them. At the end of the day, though, after their wedding, their reception, their short evening at the club, the most important thing to them was their seclusion. Maybe she and Sam weren't so different after all.

He explored her features with grateful wonder. "Think we'll be canceling this season's bookings?"

"I think Knox will be lucky if Jane lets him leave the island before she's pregnant."

"Knowing Knox, she won't have to ask."

"Of course she won't," she said, pushing him onto his back to tuck herself against him. "Knox knows his girl. And Toria and I may have double-checked family was what he wanted."

"Anyone would have to be blind, deaf, and dumb to mistake what Jane sees in her future."

"Mimi would love great grandchildren."

"Yeah, though I'm not so sure Thena wants to be a grandmother just yet."

"Did Caspian bring a date to the wedding?" she asked. "I didn't get a chance to catch up with him."

Or about a million other people.

She and Caspian had met in the past, sure, been in the same room more than once. They didn't have time together though. She didn't quite have a read on him where romance was concerned.

"No one serious," Z said. "Just a plus one."

Presentation and appearances.

Life could look like one thing and be something completely different. People might expect one behavior and get another. Lifestyle progressed. Someone who knew Zairn ten or fifteen years ago, and hadn't seen him since then, would probably be surprised to see what he was today.

"Do you think about it?"

"Caspian's sex life?" he asked, silently mocking her. "I think more about yours."

Tracing her hand down his ribs, she pressed her

fingers deep into his hip, then relaxed them to drum her fingertips across his groin.

"About other women."

"Do I think about other women?" And he wasn't teasing anymore. "No. Never. Why would you—"

"I don't mean as prospective partners." On a laugh, she boosted up to land her forehead on his for a second before rearing back. "You will never, ever get better than me, baby."

"So why would I think about other women?"

"It's not the women, I guess, it's the lifestyle. Women were a huge part of your life. Different ones, every night for ten, fifteen years."

"I gave that life up a long time before you."

"I know, but before me, you still had the prospect of enjoying different women. Now there's nothing but me in your nights."

"Do you think about other men?"

Her grin did little to hide her amusement. God, she was giddy, this relationship gave more happiness than she ever could have imagined.

"That's different."

"Always different, Ms. Kyst." He squeezed her waist when she sat up on him. "Enlighten me. Why is it different?"

"I've had one-night stands. A handful of them, maybe. You've had literally thousands of women."

"You want the world's highest scorer, you're looking for a Dunridge."

She shook her head, leaning forward until her hair cascaded around them. "You must've thought about it. Did you ever think you'd be here? One pussy for the rest of your life? You will never pick up another woman, never learn about her for the first time, never kiss her for the first time."

Catching her hair between his fingers, it gathered

as he grasped her cheeks. "But I will have all my lasts… with you. That is something to cherish. Something far more valuable than any hollow hook-up." The warmth in the deep blue of his eyes drew her in, mesmerizing her. Not one ounce of doubt. Only gratitude. Appreciation. "That part of my life was over a long time ago. Since then, I've been looking for you."

"For me?"

"Didn't know your name back then, but you were the woman I was waiting for."

Her eyes closed slowly as she blew out a slow breath. "Man, you're smooth."

"Reserved for you, baby."

"And you already got in my pants, you are dedicated." Rocking her hips over his, she moved like their connection was intimate. Her fingertips slid down his body until they were near the center of hers, and the thickening truth of his arousal for her. "We need a word."

"What kind of a word? A safe word?"

"A sex word."

"We can never have enough of those."

"Something we can say when we want to be alone," she said. "Roxiverse means cameras. Are you sure you want this?"

"You are good at what you do, Lo. Amazing." No hesitation. "We've done this before. We started like this. Only difference now is they know you're the star."

"*They* know?"

"Oh, I always knew you were the more captivating of the two of us. The world wants you and I can't blame them."

"You know this isn't about fame."

"They can't get enough of you, baby. I identify with that too. Everything you are is me, is us. And I'm proud to stand beside you. I love to see you shine. I love to see you out there, doing your thing, and knowing…”

“Knowing?”

“You come home to me and I get you all to myself.”

The spread of her smile stretched. “We’re just so perfectly suited.”

“Exactly what I’ve been saying.”

“We should get married or something.”

Again, he swept her hair aside to see more of her. “You make the rules, Lola,” he said. “You want it to stop, change, you have the wheel. And if you need me to step in—which you won’t because you’re you—know I’ll respect and fight for whatever you decide.”

“I promised it wouldn’t get in the way of us or your work.”

“It’s a natural progression from your streams. Your popularity is soaring, to maximize that exposure you need an easily accessible global outlet. Somewhere everyone can find you. Do you remember my single condition?”

“Additional security, I remember.”

“You said you wouldn’t fight me on this. Your safety remains my responsibility. What I say goes, huh?”

“Yes, what you say goes.” She meant to restrain her eye roll, honestly, she did. Somehow it slipped out of its own accord. “We’ll have guests who have their own security and I’m more than covered in the club.”

“No excuses, this is a dealbreaker.”

And although she might like to tell him that her choices were her choices, this wasn’t a time to be stubborn for the sake of it. They were in this honesty and respect zone that prompted her to pause for breath. Something she couldn’t be accused of always doing.

“No excuses.”

“I won’t always be around.” Because they weren’t always in the same place. “Who are your guests?”

"We've got some big names," she faux boasted. "And some old faces. Do you remember Bree?"

"The blonde you wanted to sleep with, yes." His serious delivery earned him a shove, but his smile was a quick, defusing follow up. "And Jill."

She'd be impressed, except he somehow never forgot anyone.

"You know we joke about Bree, but Dale actually did want to sleep with me."

"Never heard of him. I already forgot his name."

Remembered he forgot?

Licking her lips, she laughed. "You never feel threatened. Never. Not even a tiny bit."

"Should I be threatened?"

She trailed a fingertip down his torso, snaking it left and right. "No, of course not. I actually…"

"Say it, Roxanna."

"I like it. I love the power of our relationship. I love how I never look at another woman and think you might be tempted. It's never occurred to me you might be. And I love the strength of your ego, Casanova. That you can see me with other guys and never think for a moment it means anything."

"I have a healthy ego," he said, stroking her arms as her fingers kept running across his flesh. "But the security of our relationship has nothing to do with ego. You love me, Roxanna, and I trust you. Hell, even that isn't the right word because it suggests you're resisting something. We just are and there's no one else."

"God, I want to marry you."

He laughed. "Again? Already. You did say we had to rehearse for a potential naked wedding."

"Everything you say sounds like wedding vows."

Seizing her waist, he snatched her tight. "You never say that when I'm inside you."

Shit. She shivered. Because the things he said

should be reserved for a naked wedding… with zero guests and one big bed.

"Usually, I can't form thoughts, let alone words, when you're talking to me like that. Give a girl a chance."

"Back to business?" he said with a semi-side nod, his head still in the pillow. "So you're getting the other finalists back?"

"And some of the Experience winners."

"None of whom will have their own security teams."

"Thena and Mimi will guest star too."

"That should be interesting."

Thena and Mimi were Knox Collier's mother and grandmother, respectively. Hollywood heavyweights. And that might tempt Jane to poke her head around the camera once or twice.

"We have a sort of transition from the documentary to the show. There will be interview segments. We'll have Queens and Delights and Crimsettes. It will feature a lot of women supporting women, maybe like an agony aunt thing where we solve problems and help people regain their strength."

"Other than being perfect for you, that's a worthy cause."

"We may slip in Lola's Liberty and Huddle Hope where we can too. Alice and I were talking about Tripp representing Lighting Darkness."

"What does Tripp say to that?"

Her whole body shrug cast off the question. "I don't think anyone's told him yet."

Though it would be no surprise if he'd somehow divined it.

"Be careful putting Tripp Breckenridge in front of a camera, Lola."

"You think he'll outshine me?"

"No, but the guy already knows everyone. His

fame is sort of underground right now. You amp that up, he won't be able to do what he does the way he does it anymore."

And she hadn't considered that. "Huh…" she pondered.

"You'll be in the club?"

"Yeah, we'll have some behind the scenes stuff. Tours for sneak peeks, event planning, contests. And some of the fun stuff at night."

"People expect it."

"We'll slip in drinks or lunches and pamper sessions if and when it's appropriate."

"And in New York?"

"You don't have to worry. I promised this wouldn't get in the way of your work and it won't. I'll keep the customers coming, you keep the corporate wheels turning."

"I want to support you."

"This is you supporting me. You can be around, sporadically, briefly, where appropriate, but you don't have to take on any of the responsibility… Unless they need to catch me making out with anyone. In which case, I'll call Tibbs."

"Wonder how he'll put that in the diary. More future planning?"

"That's the great thing about being married." Lying down on him again, she stretched her arms as her hands slid up over his shoulders. "You can tell people you have plans with your fabulous wife."

"She is fabulous. What else can I use that for?"

"Whatever you want. Now I'm the ball and chain, just roll your eyes and they'll figure I'm nagging you."

"You're forgetting you're beautiful, smart, sassy, sexy." His words rumbled in her hair. "I say I've got plans with my wife, and it doesn't involve laying you down somewhere imminently, I'll have to return my guy card." What a sweetie. "You love that we're not jealous? I love that every other fucker on the planet is. There's not a guy you couldn't have, Roxanna."

"I could probably have some women too."

"No probably about it. Shame I don't share."

She hummed against him. "Someone is looking for a treat…" Kissing his throat, his chest, she went higher to his jaw while her arm outstretched to snag his cellphone from the nightstand. "Let's order from that seafood place we love."

"After," he growled, trying to take the phone.

Sitting up, she laughed. "We order now, and it'll be here just when we're done."

"There is no done with you."

That was a fair point. They had the ability and means to hole themselves up forever. Neither of them had to work another day in their life and they'd still die in luxury. As would their staff and their children, and their children's children. Unless something or someone intervened, they may never leave.

"You'll have to charge the phone for a bit before it will come on." Something she had vast experience with. "Trust an expert."

"It's not dead," he said, taking it from her to press the power button. "It's just off."

She feigned ignorance. "Huh, I didn't know they did that."

"Stick with me, kid."

The screen merged into his focus. Giving him space, a little, she switched back to her own side of the bed. Geez, he was sexy, even watching him read turned her on. Those eyes, so intent, she ran her fingers into his hair. In her peripheral vision, the color of the screen changed and the device went crazy. Beeping, flashing, pinging. Combing her fingers through his locks again, she wriggled closer to rest her mouth on his arm.

"You could always take your best girl out for dinner."

"Like a date?" he asked, his thumb moving across the screen, brow absorbed. "I'm a married man."

She pressed her lips deeper into his flesh. "But, Mister, you promised to make me a big star."

Despite the expression of innocence and the Marilyn voice, her laugh bubbled out when his head rolled and he crooked an eyebrow at her.

"Baby, you're already a star in my eyes."

She sat up. "Was this my audition?"

"Yeah." He vaulted up, kissing her forehead a second before he was upright. "We'll pick it up again in a minute."

The phone went to the nightstand, and he disappeared into the closet, which probably meant the bathroom. In a minute? There'd be a call, or he'd respond to a text, maybe an email, one thing would follow another. She exhaled and lay down. Her guy was seriously in demand. Though she loved being the only thing in his world, she also liked him to be out there, busy, loving her anyway.

The water went on in the bathroom. Yep, he was washing up. If she went in there… Mmm… Ideas…

Z's cellphone rang, so she scooted over to see if it was anyone she might want to talk to.

"Ah, Carolyn," she said after reading the name on the screen and picking up. "Zairn's in the shower."

"I was looking for you."

"Oh…" She sat up, finger-combing her hair, like that would make a difference to her manic mop. "Is everything okay?"

"Are you still in Los Angeles?"

"Yes, we are."

While her friend didn't sound worried or scared,

there was somewhat of an urgency to her words. Might even be excitement.

Carolyn exhaled. "Would you meet me for lunch?"

"Sure!" So it was lunchtime? Good to know. "Want me to leave Zairn behind?"

"If you wouldn't mind. You're newlyweds, I know that—"

"Don't worry about it," Roxie said. "Absence makes the heart grow fonder and all that…" She lowered her volume and pitch. "And, between you and me, that guy's itching to check his emails."

Businessy stuff had taken a backseat for too long. Her guy needed his groove to truly appreciate every second with her.

"Thank you," Carolyn said. "There's someone I'd like you to meet."

"Hmm, intriguing. I'm always on board for intrigue."

"I'll send the location to your phone."

Zairn's phone, her phone, all one and the same.

After hanging up, she pounced out of bed and went through to the bathroom. The shower was on, but Zairn was at the mirror with his shaver.

"Miss me already?"

"I need first shower." Without delay, she hurried in and soaked her hair. "I'll be quick."

"This is my shower," he said and slid open the screen to join her. "The shower I warmed up."

"What's yours is mine." She snagged the shampoo, but he quickly swiped it from her and returned it to the shelf. "I have a date before our date. If you want sex, you better get yours quick."

And from how he crowded her into the corner with that feral look on his face, that's exactly what he wanted.

"A date, huh?" His wet hand slithered up her side. Despite the hot water, little chilled sparkles darted beneath her skin. "That's something you should tell your husband."

"It's with an older woman…" She draped her arms over his shoulders. "And she's married too."

"Swinging already?"

"Would that get you going, Casanova?"

"Anything you do gets me going."

He bowed for a kiss, but she pulled back, using her anchor on him for balance.

"People assume you must be a depraved, perverted playboy living a debauched life."

"Mm hmm."

Her teeth dragged on her lower lip. "Let's not disappoint them."

One life. Theirs. From then on, there would be no other. With him, everything made sense and there was no such thing as overwhelmed. Other than by her love for him. One man had changed her life, her outlook, commanded her sanity. And what did he want in return? Utter love and devotion. That wasn't too much to ask, not when she demanded the same in return.

This was what happily ever after felt like… about damn time.

THERE'S MORE TO COME FROM THE ROXIVERSE…

Thank you for reading this tale!
If you can, please take the time to review.

~

Ask your local library for more Scarlett Finn novels!

~

For all things Scarlett Finn
check out:

www.scarlettfinn.com

NOTHING TO
TELL
SCARLETT FINN